I0680518

CROAKIES MONSTER

SAM CHEEVER

ELECTRIC PROSE PUBLICATIONS

Ancient Chinese proverb says, give cat mouse and give frog fly, they'll soothe your monsters so you won't die.

Okay, maybe I just made that up. But I'll try anything at this point.

Croakies is suddenly being overrun by monsters. Yeah. Monsters. And I have no clue where they're coming from. Are they tied to something we've done in the past? Do they have anything to do with the strange phone calls I've been getting from a really prickly local author? Most importantly, how are we going to explain to the humans about the appearance of a certain giantnormous blue monster flinging car-sized cookies around? Where did all these squirrel squattin' songbirds come from? And, for the love of the goddess's favorite spanks, why is there ice all over the floor?

Sigh.

The frog and the cat? Yeah, they're really pretty useless on this one. But at least they're living the good life thanks to my tireless efforts to feed, house, and clean up after them and their naughty friend Hobs.

Yay me.

Mega monster boogers! This magic wrangling gig is for the birds. And the frogs. And the cats. And the hobgoblins. And, apparently, for the monsters hiding at Croakies.

CLANG-G-G-G-G-G!

lang, clang, clangggggggggg...

I rubbed my forehead, trying to soothe the perpetual headache caused by the nearly constant clanging of new orders popping up, and reached out a hand to catch the sheet of paper drifting downward from thin air.

I caught the page without looking at it and shoved it to the bottom of the growing pile on top of Shakespeare's desk.

Sebille came up behind me, stuffing another thin stack of orders beneath the one I'd just received.

I sighed wearily.

Clangggggggggg...

Thank goodness Lea had found a way to mute the sound of new orders arriving, or I'd have gone totally batty from the almost unending barrage. It seemed that whatever we'd done during our recent trek to the dimensional buffer Plex had realigned something in the Universe and a backlog of artifact collection orders I hadn't even known existed had come unclogged and were burying me in work.

Clangggggggg...

I made notes on the order I was currently reviewing and added it to a folder of ten retrievals I planned to attempt as soon as I had my breakfast.

Sebille would leave Croakies with another ten orders. With any luck, we'd each get through half of the planned orders for the day.

Then we'd get a few hours of sleep and start all over again.

Clangggggggg...

I fought despair, feeling as if I was going to die buried under a pile of magical artifact orders.

My head shot up at the sound of a high-pitched screech, surprising a small yelp out of me. Hobs slid past, feet spread and arms akimbo as if he were skiing down a mountainside. His blue eyes were wide and alight with pure joy as he slid past me, my cat Mr. Wicked hot on his trail.

I turned in my chair and watched as Hobs lost his balance and, feet sliding around underneath him, toppled sideways and landed hard in Casanova's perverted chair. A beat later, he flinched, flew into the air, and crashed back into the chair with another shriek of joy. "Again!"

Shaking my head, I turned away. I picked up the

folder I'd been filling with orders and stood, stretching my aching muscles. I'd been working almost non-stop, twenty-hour days, trying to get caught up on the backlog of orders. My vision was blurry and my bones were tired and I had a brand-new array of bumps, bruises, and scratches from my efforts.

My gaze slid to the pile of new magical artifacts across the library. Sebille and I had started out organizing them carefully on top of a thirty-foot-long special wooden artifact table that usually stood mostly empty. But as we'd become overwhelmed, we'd quickly fallen into the "smile and pile" method, and the table was looking pretty chaotic at the moment.

"Again!" Hobs yelled as the chair pinched his scrawny bottom, and he leaped into the air with a delighted shriek.

Wicked was tucked into a prim sitting position at the bottom of the chair, feet neatly arranged near his fuzzy bottom and tail wrapped tidily around them. His head lifted and lowered each time Hobs made the trip from chair to air and back down again.

I bit down on the desire to scream at the boisterous hobgoblin. It wasn't his fault I was tired and cranky. He was just having a little fun.

I took a step toward the stairs leading to my apartment above Croakies, my mind already on the retrieval jobs ahead. My foot slipped out from under me.

I gave my own little shriek as my feet slid apart, and I went down, arms akimbo and papers sailing out of the folder to fall around me like giant, rectangular snowflakes.

I lay there with my legs splayed in painful splits and groaned as I took stock.

Headache: blazing. Back: aching. Legs: screaming. Arms: shaking.

Yep, all body parts accounted for.

I rolled over and tried to push myself off the ground. My hand slipped over a patch of...ice?

"What in the name of the goddess's Sunday best...?"

I looked up at the sound of clomping footsteps and found Sebille frowning down at me.

"Why are you sprawled all over the floor, Naida?"

Compassion thy name is Sebille.

"I fell. Slipped actually. On this patch of ice."

Sebille narrowed her iridescent green gaze. "What ice?"

"This ice right here..." I ran my hand over the spot where the ice had been, and it was gone. "I swear it was here a minute ago."

Sebille scoffed. "Sure it was. Somebody needs to get more sleep, I think."

She wasn't wrong. I was dead tired.

Shaking my head, I pushed upright. "I'm going to

go take a shower and have a really strong cup or three of tea. We should get going early today, that Groundhog Day alarm clock artifact is set to go off at nine AM." I gathered up the orders I'd dropped. "Some poor derf is about to relive Groundhog Day for about the fiftieth time." I felt his or her pain. In fact, I was starting to feel as if my life at Croakies was its own version of Groundhog Day.

Croakies Day.

Magical Cluster Day.

Clanggggggggg...

Clanging Croakies Cluster Day.

Rinnnnnggggggg...

Well, that was different. My cell phone lit up and I grabbed it, seeing an unknown number on the screen. "Croakies Bookstore," I answered, my attention scattered.

"Hello, is this the proprietress of the bookstore?"

I didn't recognize the voice. It was male and soft-spoken, the speech pattern precise and cultured. I also detected a slight English accent.

"This is Naida Griffith. How can I help you?" I expected the man to ask me if I could order a certain book for him or if I had a specific volume in stock. Those were the usual questions I got from customers. But his response surprised me.

"My name is Archibald Pudsnecker."

He hesitated a moment as if the name should mean something to me. It didn't. So, when it appeared he wasn't going to go on until I responded, I said, "It's a pleasure, Mr. Pudsnecker."

I could almost hear his disgust through the line. "Yes. Well. I'm an author. Recently relocated to Enchanted. And I'm very well-known," he added that last as if chastising me for not knowing him.

"Oh, that's wonderful. What genre do you write?"

Air hissed through the line as if he'd sighed, long and disgusted. "You own a bookstore, Ms. Griffith. I'm surprised you don't know about my books. Perhaps Croakies isn't the best vehicle for my purposes after all."

Another artifact order sifted downward. Without thinking, I reached out and snagged it. "I'm sorry, Mr. Pudsnecker..." I grimaced at the name. I couldn't imagine an author saddling himself with that name if he was trying to gain readership. "I'm in a bit of a crisis right now. If you could come to the point of what you need, I'll..."

"Never mind," he told me shortly, clearly disgusted. The call was severed with brutal efficiency, and I was left listening to dead air.

"Alrighty then," I muttered. Sighing, I headed for the showers. I couldn't control much of my life, but I *could* turn on a very hot shower and scrape off some of the detritus of the previous day.

Clangggggggggg...

I didn't even turn around as another order appeared from thin air and sifted downward. I'd pick up the pile of orders that came in later. When I got back.

Jingle…

I stopped abruptly, realizing that had been a different type of ringing noise than the one I'd been hearing for the last several days. Or the ringing inside my head.

"Can you get that, Sebille?"

Silence.

"Sebille?"

Nothing.

Expelling air in a burst of frustration, I turned to head back downstairs. "I'll get it. Don't worry about me. I'll just do everything around here," I murmured crankily.

Stomping through the door dividing the library from the store, I took my bad mood across the bookstore and peered through the window to the person who was standing on my doorstep. The street light behind him cast my visitor in an orb of white light that pushed the dark of a too-early morning to the background.

My pulse picked up, and my eyes went wide.

The man on the other side gazed back at me for a beat and then lifted his dark brows as I continued to stare without opening the door.

I shook off my shock and unlocked the deadbolts, sending my keeper energy into the magical deadbolt that backed up all the physical ones, and pulled the door open just enough to stick my face through the crack.

Detective Wise Grym looked at me, his jaw tight as he noted my lack of manners. My heart pity-patted as I took in the broad shoulders, rock-like square jaw, and thick mass of mahogany brown hair over a well-shaped head.

"Hey," I said to the too-handsome detective, a.k.a. gargoyle.

"Hey," he said back. "Can I come inside?"

I might have grimaced at the request because I saw him flinch, his dark-caramel gaze tightening with irritation. "It's business," he clarified.

Like that would make me feel better. Grym and I had been friends. Good friends. Moving toward more than friends. But then I'd discovered that he'd turned me in to the Société of Dire Magic, a regulating and monitoring body for the magical community, not once, but several times, when I'd temporarily lost control of a few magical artifacts.

As a magic-using member of the Enchanted Police Department, it had been his job to fill out those reports.

As my friend and someone who'd fought beside me when powers stronger than either of us threatened our friends and Enchanted, he should have found a way around writing those reports.

That was my opinion. Wrong or right. I was having trouble getting past my feelings to forgive him. I reluctantly stepped back and let the detective come inside Croakies.

He looked around, his gaze going soft as if he were remembering the last time he'd been there. Christmas at Croakies. When we'd all fallen victim to a pair of skinwalkers. It had been a wild ride, but in the end it had turned into one of the best Christmases I'd ever had.

Which wasn't saying all that much since I generally hated the entire last three months of the year. Magically speaking that is. When one deals in rogue magical artifacts, the holidays are generally chaotic, dangerous, and exhausting.

"What's up?" I asked, shoving my hands into the pockets of my fuzzy robe.

He scanned a look over my robe and slippers and grinned.

Sebille had given me the slippers for Christmas. They looked like gray kittens, with perky ears, long whiskers and orange eyes, representing my favorite cat. I grinned down at them. "My Christmas gift from the sprite."

He laughed. "They look like Wicked. I like them."

"So do I." There was a moment of awkward silence between us. I glanced longingly toward the dividing door, wanting to make my escape upstairs for that hot shower and a boatload of tea. It didn't look like I was going to get that shower any time soon. But I could still have the tea.

"I was just getting ready to make tea. You want some?"

Grym shook his head. "No, thanks. There isn't time..."

Grumbly gargoyle gristle! No tea either. My day was taking a deep dive right into the dumpster.

"I need your help on a case," the detective told me. "I think there's a monster loose in Enchanted."

2

NOT FOR THE MAN BOOBS ON THE COVERS?

I usually don't like starting my day crawling around in the grass. Especially when the grass was still damp from the previous night's rain. And despite the fact that I could no longer hear the clang of artifact orders appearing from thin air, I still felt the addition of every new order like surplus tension thrumming through my nerves.

The worst part was that I never even got the cup of tea and donut I'd been hoping to talk Grym into. Since the park was only a couple of miles from Croakies, we hadn't passed any stores containing either or both.

"Anything?"

I glanced up as Grym walked over to me, his expression hopeful.

Shaking my head, I pushed to my feet. I brushed

my knees off and then rubbed my hands over my jeans. "Not a single hair. You?"

Frowning, he shook his head.

"Maybe it was just a prank call," I offered, though I doubted the cop would be so convinced of the monster's existence on the basis of one call.

His unhappy response told me I was right.

"If the thing hadn't been sighted in several different places at a variety of times, I'd probably agree with you. But we've gotten a dozen calls from homes and businesses around the park reporting a monster sighting." He grimaced.

Grym was one of only a few supernormal members of the Enchanted Police Department. He generally volunteered for any of the cases his human boss jokingly referred to as WOAS, so he could control the amount and type of information the humans received. Grym had explained to me that the acronym stood for, weird, oddball, or alien stuff. I had a strong feeling he'd cleaned that last word up for me.

Whatever you called it, though, having a super-normal running around Enchanted not apparently caring if it was seen, was worrying.

"It was spotted right here by three different people." Grym pointed to the tree line about thirty yards away. "The reports said it turned and melted into those trees over there."

"Melted?" I said, grinning. "Somebody's got a poet's soul."

Grym chuckled. "I don't think so. They described it as actually melting."

"Like ice on hot pavement kind of melting?"

Grym's lips twitched. "Now who's the poet?"

I shook my head. "The ground's too frozen for footprints. Did the reports describe this thing?"

"Over eight feet tall, long silver hair, big face with massive teeth." He grinned. "I'm pretty sure the big teeth thing might have been a bit of hysteria talking."

"Like a silver bigfoot?"

"Yeah. That was the impression I got." He frowned. "Except for the melting part. I've never heard of a melting sasquatch."

My eyes went wide. "You've heard of a sasquatch?"

"Of course. Haven't you?"

I was saved from having to answer when his phone rang.

He answered on the second ring. "Grym." He listened for a beat, his handsome face darkening in a frown. "Where?" Grym started moving toward the woods. "I'm close. I'll take the call."

I fell in behind him, glad I'd finally started being serious about getting into shape. My job had become a lot more strenuous than I'd expected, and I was tired of dragging around after artifacts with my tongue flapping in the wind, wheezing like an asthmatic gorilla.

Grym disconnected. "Another sighting. It's through the woods. Faster just to go on foot. You up to running?" He didn't wait for me to respond. He took off like a shot, leaving me to follow as best I could.

The woods was deeper than I'd thought. Darker. The trees grew increasingly closer together until we had to slow down or risk breaking an ankle on the bulging roots and tangled vines that dipped from tree to tree.

The overarching canopy of branches grew thicker too, strangling out what little sunlight managed to make it through the vegetation. Grym and I slowed to a fast walk, picking our way through the tangle of growth impeding our progress.

I was panting, itchy, and imagining all sorts of things crawling on me by the time Grym stopped abruptly ahead of me. I was scratching a big red bump, thinking about how sweaty I was, and ran into him so hard I fell backward, landing in a prickly green plant with a grunt of pain.

"Sorry about that," I told the cop.

He didn't say anything.

I shoved ungracefully to my feet. "I really hope there's no poison ivy or anything in that bush."

Grym didn't speak. He didn't move.

That was when I noticed the tension in his broad

shoulders. I moved up beside him and stopped, my pulse spiking to my ears. "Um..."

Beside me, Grym swallowed hard. One of his big hands was hovering above the gun holstered on his hip like an old Western gunslinger. His gaze was locked on the creature standing a dozen yards away from us, the sun a semi-circle, like a halo, behind its head.

I was pretty sure eight feet tall was an understatement. The monster had to be thirteen feet at least, give or take a foot. The thing was covered in long, silvery-white hair. Not fur. The silky hair covered its entire form, from its elongated head, over its extended torso, and down arms and legs that were as long as I was tall, to cover its hands and pool around its feet.

The face was covered in shorter hair, dark in the low light. But there were long, feathery brows drooping along the back corner of its small eyes, making the monster look sad. The eyes that peered at us from beneath the brows were black, but they sparked silver in the thin ribbons of sun shining down on its silky head.

The ground was glossy with ice beneath its feet, as if the monster created frost wherever it walked.

We stared at it for several moments.

It stared back at us.

I started to wonder who was going to break the stand-off first. My phone rang, the ring tone from

Dance of the Sugar Plum Fairy, which told me it was my assistant, Sebille.

And when I blinked, the tall, willowy form ahead of us seemed to melt sideways and disappear.

I looked at Grym. He looked at me.

"It melted away," I said, amusement coloring my voice.

He shook himself out of the stupor first, striding quickly toward the spot where the monster had been. And I answered my phone. "You aren't going to believe what Grym and I just saw," I said by way of greeting.

"You wanna bet?" The bushes behind where the monster had been standing rustled. Grym's hand shot toward his holster and drew the big gun, pointing it at the rustling branches.

The sprite stepped out of the trees, hands in the air. "Don't shoot, Tex."

Grym expelled air. "You should have announced yourself, Sebille. I could have shot you."

"Sorry," said the sprite in a tone that told everyone there she wasn't really. "I was a little discombobulated from discovering that the artifact I've been hunting was actually a giant Winter Monster."

I scrunched up my face. "Winter Monster? What's that?"

Beside me, Grym sighed. "Someone's imagination gone wild."

Sebille nodded. "It's tied to an artifact and can take whatever form the person who owns the artifact thinks up. Usually, it's a mix of several monsters."

"What does the artifact look like?" I asked my assistant.

She shrugged. "The order we got on the thing says it's a book. Probably a novel. Sometimes they come as videos. I remember hearing about one that was a song." She grimaced. "That was a bad one. It was a cross between a dragon and a saber tooth tiger."

Grym winced. "I remember that too. As I recall, that thing killed a couple of cops and several civilians before it was stopped."

"So, they're dangerous?" I asked, feeling fear grow.

"Think about what you read in those paranormal romance books you like so much," Sebille said. "People's imagination is only limited by what they see in the world around them. And between books, movies, and television, that's not very limited."

I flushed, carefully avoiding Grym's gaze. I really hadn't wanted anyone, especially him, to know that I liked romance books. "I just buy them for the words," I muttered sheepishly.

Grym barked out a laugh. "Not for the man boobs on the covers?"

"Moobs," Sebille said, waggling her fire-red brows.

Glaring at the sprite, I shrugged, not wanting to lie right to Grym's face. I settled, instead, for changing the subject. "Okay. In this case, I guess we're looking for a Yeti type critter. "I frowned. "Why are these called Winter Monsters? What if it was a giant scorpion from the desert?"

"It's not a seasonal thing," Grym explained. "Jedediah Winter was the man who discovered their existence, so he gets credit for them."

"Ah," I said.

"And it's a Yeti right now, but it could be that giant scorpion you mentioned tomorrow. Like I said, it changes according to its owner's inclinations. We have two choices for fixing this. We either need to find the person behind the Monster, or we need to find the artifact itself."

"Either way, we should end up at the same place, right?" I said.

"Yeah. But we can divvy up the search that way. I can take the artifact, and you can take the person."

I thought that sounded like a good plan. With all three of us working on it, we should be able to find it more quickly. "Deal." I pulled out my phone and dialed a number.

"Who are you calling," Grym asked.

"Lea," I said as my friend came on the phone. I swung my gaze to Grym and he pursed his lips before nodding his understanding. "Grym and I need your help with something. Can you come to Enchanted Park?"

L ea shivered violently, her teeth clacking together as she pulled her coat close. "I can't believe I let you talk me into this," she groused as she relit the thick, white pillar candle she'd brought for the fifth time.

"Sorry," I said, my own teeth clacking together. "It wasn't this cold when I called you."

The winter storm had blossomed out of nowhere. The sun that had threaded its way through the thick tree cover just an hour earlier was hidden behind a heavy bank of charcoal-gray clouds. The temps had dropped a good twenty degrees at its loss.

Wind scoured over us, singing a sad melody of cold and desolation as it flowed through the trees. I could smell snow on the air and the tiny flurries that were sifting down on us were coming faster and growing larger by the minute. "Maybe we should come back tomorrow."

Lea sniffed, shaking her head. "As much as I'd love to do that, the trail will be cold by then." She laughed. "Icy, in fact."

I huddled deeper into my coat and looked up as Grym returned. His face, which looked like it was carved from granite and sometimes was, had been chapped red from the cold, and his hands were purple. "No sign of the monster or an artifact." He glanced at me. "Any chance you could be wrong?"

I shook my head. Since gaining my full Keeper powers, I'd been hitting the books, learning as much as I could about artifact wrangling so that I'd be better at my job. It didn't hurt that I had the Société of Dire Magic keeping a close eye on me, watching for me to make another mistake.

I tried not to let that sobering thought show on my face as I looked at Grym. Since I still mostly blamed him for siccing them on me in the first place.

It helped a little that Grym had been responsible for getting Agent Rogers of the Société to back off a bit. However, I was under no illusions that Rogers would continue to give me space if I messed up again.

"Any products of an artifact can only be released within a two-mile radius of the artifact's location. So, unless the person who owns the book is driving around town with it, we should be able to isolate a subsection of Enchanted where the person lives."

"Then we just need to narrow it down," Grym said, nodding. "I'm not sure how we're going to do that. I guess we can go door-to-door and have you use your power to call the artifact to you."

I saw two problems with that scenario. First, if a non-magic human owned an artifact but didn't know it was magical, we'd be introducing magical knowledge where it hadn't been before. That, I knew, was against the Société of Dire Magic's laws for magic use. I smiled at the thought of turning Grym in for that. But I quickly muted the smile when he narrowed his gaze at me.

And the second problem was that I might call a lot of artifacts that rightfully belonged to people. Then we'd have to sort through all of them to figure out which one was our Winter Monster artifact.

Given the fact that I was already ear-deep in rogue artifacts I needed to find, the idea of adding twenty-fold to my backlog was not appealing.

"Okay, I'm ready," Lea said. She looked up at Grym and pointed to a spot near the circle she'd made with salt. "Can you stand there to block the wind? It keeps blowing my candles out and breaking my circle."

Grym obliged her, his bulk doing a pretty good job of protecting the circle. Lea looked at me and pointed to a spot on her other side. "Naida, you stand there."

She stepped into the sphere and picked up the container of salt, finishing off her circle. Sprawled in the center of the circle, her belly exposed and her paws batting at a small stick on the ground beside her, Lea's cat Hex seemed happy to be in the park, her thick, soft gray coat apparently doing a better job of keeping her warm than mine was doing for me.

"Let's get to work, Hex," Lea said. She kneeled next to the unlit white candle at the center of the circle and struck a match, protecting it with her hand as she held it down to the wick. The candle took a moment to light, but as soon as it did, there was a sound like air being pulled from an enclosed space, and visible lines of energy shot up from the circle and into the trees high above.

The wind inside the circle dropped away, apparently blocked by Lea's magic. She began to chant and Hex stood beside her, tail whipping the air and narrow chest glowing under the power of her particular sigil, which was the symbol to focus energy. Hex was from the same litter as Mr. Wicked. His sigil was a soul star and the other cats carried sigils representing an athame, a pentacle, and one for chaos magic.

As Lea chanted, pale green energy rose from the ground inside the circle and lifted into the air, filling the magic cylinder she'd created into the trees and beyond. I knew when the power had reached the top of her circle because it exploded outward with a muffled boom and formed a visible ring of pale green energy in the sky.

Then Lea threw her hands into the air, and the ring broke apart, shooting across the sky with a hissing sound.

We waited for the magic to locate the monster's

path, hoping it would lead us to the artifact that had spawned it.

We heard the hiss of magic searing a path through the woods a moment later. The soft, green glow danced through the trees as we watched, waiting expectantly.

With a final violent sizzle, the energy left the trees and slammed into Lea's circle. The energy surrounding her and Hex trembled, rolling over itself as it adjusted to the concussive force of her returning probe, and then settled into the circle with a sigh.

Lea lowered her hands and the cylinder above our heads dropped into a simple, glowing ring on the ground. She stretched her leg and broke the circle with a scuff of her toe.

The energy went dark, leaving only the faint scent of ozone behind.

The three of us stared at the meandering green glow snaking through the woods.

"Is that the path?" Grym finally asked. He frowned. "That's where Sebille came out of the woods."

He was right. It could very well be the sprite's path.

Lea turned to look at him, her pretty face a study in worry. "I don't know. Without a targeting object, the energy doesn't recognize the difference between one magic-user or another." She pointed to a glossy puddle of energy a few feet away from us. "And I have no idea what that is."

My gaze caught on the puddle and I sighed. "I think I do."

It was the exact spot the monster had "melted" away. And I was very afraid it was the only path that meant anything in our search.

Unfortunately, it didn't lead anywhere we could follow.

3

WILFREDA THE WITCH GOES WALKIES

"*M*aybe it's a giant worm monster," Sebille offered unhelpfully around a bite of taco.

I shook my head, observing a record-player that drew the listener back to the date of the music's creation and stranded them there until a more recent record was played. Setting it aside to catalog later, I turned to Sebille. "No, this monster looked like a Yeti, only it was white." I frowned. "Like the abominable snowman."

"Isn't that just a children's story?"

I shrugged. "Most of those stories are based on real things." But I'd researched as many Winter Monsters as I could find records for, and nothing of the kind Grym and I saw was described. "It's possible this is a completely new one. Never before seen or documented."

"That seems unlikely," Sebille said, crumpling her taco wrapper and shoving it into the bag in front of her. She sighed wearily. "I retrieved the pen that writes in musical notes and the toothbrush that cleans up potty mouth." She pointed to the end of the long table. "They're down there somewhere."

I nodded, glancing toward the spot she indicated. The pile of artifacts was daunting and it made me depressed. "We're going to need a bigger table." At my words, the thirty-foot-long artifact table grew another five feet. Pretty soon, we were going to need an annex at Croakies to accommodate it.

When the walls started to groan and shift at my thought, I blinked, panicking. "Belay that order!" The groaning stopped as the magic that controlled the size of the library backed down again. *Phew! That had been a close one.*

A soft dinging sound brought my head around. Sebille went over to the communicating mirror and tugged off the black shroud we'd been keeping on it since a doppelganger spirit tried to get a little too close to me.

Light played across Sebille's face as she waited for the caller to appear. I joined her, curious.

A few moments later, Madeline Quilleran's scary countenance appeared in the center of the glass, her living room recognizable behind her.

I caught movement in the background and snapped my gaze up to the stag on the wall above the fireplace. Felonius was its name, and I could feel it watching me whenever I came near, but I hadn't been able to catch it in the act.

"Keeper," Madeline said in her usual brisk, no-nonsense way. "Princess Sebille."

Sebille's usual resistance to being called by her magical title showed in a slight tightening of her lips, but she simply inclined her head. I was pretty sure she'd decided that, when dealing with a witch as scary as Madeline Quilleran, it was best to use every weapon you had in your arsenal.

Being the daughter of the Queen of the Fae in Enchanted was a definite plus when dealing with powerful magical creatures like the Quillerans.

The room behind Madeline erupted with the sound of fluttering wings and a large raven with small silver eyes settled to her shoulder. Madeline's familiar's name was Rasputin. The raven had a slight Russian accent and I was pretty sure he'd once been someone of great importance in what had once been the Soviet Union. Currently, he was a bird. I had no idea how that had happened but I selfishly hoped he'd been cursed for being a jerk to someone. Also, the raven didn't much like me. I didn't take it personally because I was pretty sure Rasputin hated everybody except Madeline, and maybe her young niece Maude.

The scary witch reached up and ran a fingertip over the bird's glossy black breast.

"What can we do for you, Madeline?" I asked, arching my brows at the bird as he lifted his wings and snapped his beak at me.

"I just came back from a meeting of the PTB. It's come to our awareness that there's been an explosion of artifact orders across the dimensions."

My gaze slid unhappily toward the mass of artifacts waiting to be cataloged. "Unfortunately, that's true. Sebille and I have been running ourselves ragged trying to collect them all."

Madeline looked thoughtful. "Yes. It's the same in the other dimensions. We're speculating that you opened up some kind of blockage when you interfered in that business of the gate in Plex."

I clenched my jaw at her wording. "You mean when Sebille, I, Hobs, Slimy, and Wicked saved the Universe from another Dark Rages at great risk to ourselves?"

Madeline shrugged and Ras made a chuffing sound that sounded like laughter. I glared at the stupid bird and he lifted his wings in threat, dancing across Madeline's shoulder.

"Whatever the outcome of that effort, you can't argue that something's changed. I'm calling to warn you that the flood of artifacts moving through the system has drawn the attention of the Société of Dire Magic. You can expect to hear from Agent Rogers sometime soon."

Pickled Peach pits! "That's just awesome."

"Yes. Have a nice day, Keeper. Princess."

Madeline started to sign off, but I stopped her. "How's Rustin?"

"And Sadie?" Sebille asked, frowning as if she was pretty sure she wasn't going to like the answer.

Madeline appeared surprised, as if she'd totally forgotten about them. I knew that wasn't the case. Since taking on the task of fixing Rustin after Madeline's evil brother put Rustin's soul into a frog, the Witch never seemed to forget my unfortunate friend. She'd been keeping Rustin on a short tether. "They're both fine. In fact, I think he's ready for a trial run. I told him that myself this morning. I expect you'll hear from Rustin..." she scanned Sebille a look. "Both of them...soon." She gave us a tight smile. "It sounds like you can use some help. The timing should be optimal." She disappeared without another word. My gaze shot to the elusive stag head as the screen started to darken from the edges out, and I had a brief flash of intuition that Felonius had winked at me. But when I focused on him, he was staring straight ahead. "I'm going to catch you one of these days," I told the wall decoration before the mirror went totally dark.

Had he smiled?

I looked at Sebille. "Do you believe her about Rustin and Sadie?"

"I don't know. If it was true, I would have thought they'd be here by now."

I nodded, looking at the table of artifacts. I knew I should start cataloging the mess. But I just couldn't bring myself to do it. "I still need to get that Groundhog Day alarm clock. I think I'll go see if I can mark that one off my list."

Fortunately, the number of new orders for the day had slowed to a trickle. I was pretty sure we'd only gotten five or six new ones since Grym had come by that morning and pulled me away from my work.

Sebille's gaze fell on the table, and she seemed to have the same thought I'd had. "I'll come with you. Maybe we can grab the comb that thickens hair after we get the clock."

The idea of knocking two more artifacts off my list appealed. "Let's do it." I went to grab the two orders from Shakespeare's desk and frowned. The Book of Pages was sitting on top of the order pile. I hadn't put it there. The book had a tendency to move around on its own when it was trying to tell me something. Running my fingers over the cover, I noted how the leather softened and warmed under my touch. "What are you up to?" I asked the book. But it didn't open and I figured that meant it wasn't trying to communicate anything. Sebille had probably moved it there. I turned to ask her, but she was gone. I heard her thumping around in the bookstore. Probably bundling up for the blustery weather outside.

Sighing, I headed for the dividing door.

I could hear Hobs talking animatedly through the open door to my apartment. Slimy and Wicked were up there too, the three of them were hanging out and probably plotting the destruction of the world.

"We're going out, you three. Stay out of trouble." Hobs appeared on the landing above our heads. "We will, Miss. Stay warm, there's a cold front coming."

The way he said it made my stomach tighten with dread. But when I looked into his big blue eyes, I saw no guile or mischief there. "We'll do that."

The lights overhead flickered violently as I headed toward the dividing door. I screeched to a stop, looking around.

"That's been happening a lot since we came back from Plex," I muttered to myself, thinking we must have electrical interference of some kind.

I decided to have Sebille ask her mother to come by and check it out. If there was magical influence, the Queen of the Fae in Enchanted would be just the supernormal to suss it out. Having made that decision, I opened the door.

And was nearly decapitated by a flying book.

He stood just inside the exterior door, so tall his head was only a couple of feet beneath the tiles of my thirty-foot-tall ceilings.

He appeared much bigger than he'd looked in the park.

Huddled against the wall beside the door, Sebille was wide-eyed and even paler than usual. "We have a visitor," she murmured to me, barely moving her lips.

"Yeah," I agreed on a whisper. "We certainly do."

I jerked back as a slender hardback volume shot past my head. The book pinged off the bathroom door and floated away as if suspended on a string held by a giant puppet master. I recognized the book as one of the children's titles I kept in the store. I didn't have all that many young customers at Croakies, but I had a handful of bookish young mothers who left their progeny in front of the small bookshelf unit devoted to youth books while they perused the shelves for romance and mystery books.

Sebille squeaked as a chunky cardboard picture book entitled, *Wilfreda the Witch goes Walkies*, flew straight at us. She reached up and caught the volume handily and then grunted as the book tore back out of her hand and flew away.

The monster by the door shifted slightly, sending

the stench of wet dog wafting through the store. A brisk, icy wind scoured past, blowing a pile of customer orders into the air with its breath. The sheets of paper danced to the floor in the wind's icy grip.

I shivered, wrapping my arms around myself as the blustery breezes grew colder and more animated.

A chunk of ice broke off over our heads and sliced downward, missing my head by inches and stabbing the carpet in front of my shoe.

That was when I noticed the ice covering the floor and every available surface. Icicles hung from the furniture, shelves, and sales counter and glistened along the glossy ceiling tiles overhead.

It crunched under my foot when I moved.

The thing by the door took an enormous step forward, cocked its head, and waved a hand. As if we were inside a snow globe that he'd just shaken, snow began to fall from the ceiling, drifting downward in pretty flakes the size of a fingertip.

The monster had turned Croakies into a winter wonderland. It looked around with childlike glee, smiling.

Sebille and I gulped at the sight of all those really big white teeth.

"We should probably do something," Sebille said.

"Yeah, I agree. Like what?"

The sprite shrugged. "I don't know, maybe sell it a book on how to winterize its car?"

I snorted out a laugh and the monster's head tilted again, its eyes widening slightly.

Taking a deep breath, I decided I had to be the master of my surroundings and took a step forward.

My foot slipped on the ice covering the floor, and I threw my arms out in an attempt to stay upright as I slid in a complete circle, my weight trying to pull me to the floor.

Enjoying the show, the monster didn't move.

When I'd finally mastered my balance, I stood half bent over to keep from losing it again and tried a smile. "Um, ah, welcome to Croakies. Can I...erm... help you?"

Behind me, Sebille snorted.

I whipped my head around to glare at her, and that was all it took for me to completely lose control of my body and hit the ground.

I lay sprawled for a few seconds, my heart pounding as I realized I'd inadvertently slid closer to the monster. It stared at me for a beat as I slowly lowered my hands and, ever so carefully shoved myself a few inches away.

The glacial blue gaze narrowed. The almost perfectly triangular pink nose twitched, and then the thing moved.

It was big. It was stinky. But it moved fast.

Really fast.

I squealed and rolled to my knees, crawling frantically toward Sebille as the building shook under the monster's weight.

Two strides. That was all it took for the creature to be on top of me. And when the massive hands wrapped around my waist, the thing pinched me so tightly in its grip I couldn't even draw a breath to scream.

4

MAYBE YOU COULD HELP?

*T*he monster lifted me to a spot in front of its face. I couldn't see what was happening but I felt the thing's perusal of my...well basically all he could see was my backside.

My cheeks went pink, and I mentally harangued myself for worrying about how wide my boohind looked from that vantage point. *Who in the goddess's spare galoshes cared what the Winter Monster thought about my backside?*

I mean, it wasn't like he and I were going to be dating.

I had higher standards than that.

I preferred my men only to have hair on their heads. And, their armpits, though that was just because it was generally accepted that males of the species had armpit hair. And maybe one or two other places that were generally accepted. But definitely not on his elbows. Hairy elbows were just not sexy. Or hairy knees.

Nope. No hair there either.

I shook off my thoughts. "Sebille, does he look like he's thinking of having an early dinner?"

She frowned. "It's hard to tell. His teeth are definitely showing. But he could just be laughing at your mom jeans."

"Har," I told Sebille. "Maybe you could help?" I arched my brows at her, amazed at her lack of motivation as my life hung in the balance.

Literally.

The world suddenly shifted, and I shot upward on a piercing scream. The thought flashed through my terrorized brain that he was going to eat me. But I never felt the razor sharpness of his big white teeth. Instead, I plunged downward again, screaming like a gravy-coated mouse at an alley-cat convention. I realized I was clutching the monster's massive, leathery fingers like a lifeline and tried to unclench, but then the thing lifted me toward the ceiling again and my arms clamped down of their own volition.

A deep, thundering rumble accompanied his antics and I realized the thing was laughing at me.

Awkward.

To my everlasting chagrin, Mr. Abominable shook me up and down again several more times. I was dizzy and nauseous by the time I realized it probably wasn't going to eat me, but there was a good chance it would shake me to death.

"Sebille!" I yelled as I plunged downward again. "Do something!"

"What do you want me to do? If I throw magic at the thing, it might drop you."

I glanced her way. To her credit, she did have energy dancing in her palms and a worried look on her face.

That made me feel better and worse at the same time.

Was it possible I had no options?

Then I thought of something. "I'm going to zap it when I'm close to the ground, so if it drops me, it won't hurt as much."

She frowned but nodded. "I'll try to catch you if I can."

That didn't sound very promising at all.

The monster jerked me toward the ceiling.

My stomach rebelled and I tasted bile. So not good. Even worse, my head actually brushed against an icicle there and sharp pain pierced my scalp. "Okay, new problem. He's going to skewer me on an icicle."

Sebille suddenly popped away and I panicked.

She's running? Really? "You're just going to leave me here alone?" My voice had a definite hysterical tone to it.

A burst of green light flared in front of me, and

Sebille hovered on the air in her sprite form, hands on hips and iridescent green gaze flashing anger. "Naida, do you really think so little of me?"

I would have probably said something we would both regret, but the monster's hand shot upward again and I was too busy screaming bloody murder.

Behind me, the exterior door to Croakies slammed open.

The monster's hand started to lower, and the thing began to turn.

I looked at Sebille. "Forget *me*, save whoever that is!"

She nodded and shot upward, flying right at the enormous, toothy face of the Winter Monster. "Hey, stupid!" she yelled.

The creature's gaze whipped back toward the sprite, and it roared as she charged its face, her iridescent purple and green wings buzzing so fast it was hard to see them. She shot away as a big hand slammed in her direction, and then returned again to buzz around its ears.

The monster opened its hand and let go of me so it could slap at the irritating sprite.

I knew exactly how it felt.

I sailed toward the floor, landing in a crouch as pain zinged through my knees. "Ouch!"

A huge, hairy foot flashed in my direction. I dodged around it, my thoughts focused on getting whoever had come into the store out of the building as Sebille continued to keep the monster busy.

I stopped dead in my tracks when I saw who it was. Gaze narrowing.

"Never mind, Sebille," I told my assistant. "You can let the monster eat this one."

Rogers glowered over at me, his small, slender form standing primly just inside the door. He stood with his feet tucked together at the heels, hands clasping the handle of a walking stick I was pretty sure he didn't need. The man's face was narrow and pasty, with a pointy chin that was made sharper by the dark blond goatee framing it.

As usual, Rogers wore an old-fashioned black suit with rounded lapels, a strange bowler hat covering his dark blond hair.

His nose twitched, making his mustache dance unhappily, and he held me in a derisive glare. "I see you're up to your usual tricks, Naida keeper."

The monster moved, lightning-fast, and Sebille yelped as he nearly caught her in his meaty fist.

Green light flared like camera flashes above my head.

I shrugged. "I'm not doing anything except trying to survive, Agent Rogers." I reached over and sent a thick bolt of keeper energy into the monster's foot. It bellowed, hopped up on one foot and spun, looking at me as if it was thinking about smashing me into the threadbare carpet.

I threw energy at its other foot and then gathered a thick ball of silver magic in both fists as it bellowed again. "Don't even think about it, Mister."

The monster's eyes rounded. It took one last swipe at Sebille and then, with a final roar of displeasure, the critter melted into my carpet.

Behind me, the soft plop of several books hitting the ground put a period on his departure.

I looked at Rogers. "What can I do for you, Agent Rogers?"

He looked around the bookstore, his judgmental, light-blue gaze finding every flaw and lingering there in silent accusation. Melting ice dripped from the ceiling, plopping onto the floor and the covers of the fallen books. I hurried to pick up the books, drying them on my clothes before the covers were spotted.

A soft crackling sound preceded the crashing of an icicle to the carpet, followed almost immediately by several more.

Sebille popped back to full size and grabbed two umbrellas from the closet by the tea-making counter. She handed me one and held the other over her head as she helped me pick up the books.

His lip curled, Rogers's icy blue gaze followed us around as if he were watching roaches scurrying from one pile of trash to another.

I clamped down on the defensive inclinations burning a hole in my throat. Trying to plead my case would only make me look weak. Rogers was a bully. If he sensed any weakness, he would pounce.

When the books were safe, I turned back to the door, cocking a questioning brow in his direction. I stood there waiting for him to tell me why he'd come to befoul my day.

"I understand there's an artifact in Enchanted that's creating a monster. I've also been told that you have no idea how to locate it." He jerked his head toward the spot where the monster had been. The carpet there was drenched, melted ice puddling in the shapes of two giant feet where the silver abominable had compressed the ancient padding underneath. "I've seen the results first hand. What do you think would have happened if a human customer had come through this door, Naida keeper?"

I would have been much happier to see them than I'd been to see him, I thought. "I'd have handled it." It wasn't as outrageous a statement as it seemed. Most of my customers were magic users and would have been alarmed, but not all that surprised. However, I did have a few human customers who would have been terrified if they'd seen the Winter Monster. It would have been hard to explain away the presence of the monster effectively enough to keep them from running shrieking to the newspapers about it.

A direct response was inadvisable, so I decided to pretend I hadn't heard the question. "We're on this thing's trail. I hope to have it locked down by tomorrow."

Rogers didn't look convinced, but he inclined his chin. "See that you do, Keeper. I'll be staying in town for the duration, just in case."

Oh goody. I pinched my lips closed to trap the snarky response behind them.

Agent Rogers and I stood in a silent standoff for another moment. Finally, he inclined his chin again and left.

I had to lock my jaw to keep from sticking my tongue out at him.

"Who do you suppose turned us in about the monster?" Sebille asked, her gaze on Rogers as he and his snake-headed walking stick glided past the big window at the front of the store.

My gut reaction was to blame Grym. But then I realized he'd asked for *my* help with the monster. "That's a very good question," I said, frowning.

"So," Sebille said on a sigh. "I guess I'll go get the Plex vacuum."

The Plex vacuum was one of several artifacts I'd brought back from my last adventure, when a dimensional wrinkle had sucked a few cows, a fainting goat, Hobs, Mr. Slimy, Mr. Wicked and yours truly into another dimension. Sebille and I had discovered upon returning home with the hand-held device, that it turned anything we sucked up with it into songbirds.

Really.

I had birds flying and pooping all over the artifact library. And as was my luck, they didn't seem to want to go back outside. It was, after all, still cold out there since Winter was still clinging to the streets of Enchanted.

I sighed. "I'm going to have to buy more bird food."

Sebille nodded. "It's better than soggy carpets and mold, though."

I had an idea. "We could take the birds to Lea's greenhouse. Your mother would enjoy them, right?"

"She might. As long as they don't eat her plants."

Sebille's people, the Enchanted Fae population, had been burned out of their toadstool city in the Enchanted Forest by the evil Quillerans. Not the ones who were helping our friend Rustin, but the other side of the family. The ones who stuck Rustin into a frog in the first place.

My friend, Lea had been kind enough to offer them a home in her giantnormous greenhouse, which stayed warm and comfortable all year long. The Fae were safe there. Happy. And, as an added bonus, the greenhouse was producing some of the healthiest plants and largest, sweetest fruit I'd ever tasted.

Feeling better about having a solution, I went to fetch the little vacuum cleaner. And proceeded to make myself some birds.

5

I DIDN'T WANT TO GET A MONSTROUS CAVITY

"Those birds are making me crazy," Sebille groused the next morning. "Singing, singing, all the time singing. What do they have to be so blasted happy about, anyway? They're just stupid birds."

I yawned. "I have no idea. But I do know we need to catch that monster today. The last thing we need is for Rogers to show back up again."

My phone rang and I saw that it was Grym. I answered it without wasting time on Hello. "Did you get a visit from Agent Rogers too?"

"Rogers? No, why?"

"He's staying in town until we catch the monster. He seems to think the thing's presence is all my fault."

Silence pulsed between us for a moment. I hadn't meant my words to come out sounding like an accusation. But it was clear Grym had taken them that way. I figured the best thing was to just move on. "What's up?"

"I take it you haven't seen the news?"

"No. Why?"

"Apparently, there's a giant blue monster rampaging down the streets near the capital building. Naida, it's throwing cookies at cars and people. Really big cookies. The street's a mess of wrecked cars and terrified people."

I closed my eyes, knowing I would become a target for the Société over the new development. "Please tell me you're joking?"

"Sorry. I can't do that. I'll be by in five minutes to pick you up." He disconnected without giving me a chance to argue.

"What's wrong?" Sebille asked.

I sighed. "You aren't going to believe it."

"You'd be surprised what I'll believe."

I told her what Grym had told me. She stared at me for a long moment and then smirked. "You're messin' with me, right?"

Shaking my head, I trudged upstairs to change and brush my teeth. After all, good dental hygiene is important when one intends to conquer a cookie-flinging monster. I didn't want to get a monstrous cavity.

We stood at the end of the street and stared, our mouths hanging open. Beneath my feet, the crunch of cookie crumbs was a constant refrain, the scent of sugar and chocolate chips rising to tempt and tantalize.

An enormous cookie in his hand, the monster crouched at the end of the street, near the statue of Occulas Mylantis, the wizard who'd established Enchanted and had owned much of its commerce until his "death" a hundred and fifty years earlier. The human population of Enchanted thought he'd been a great intellectual, whose love of learning had led him to invent improvements in medicine, agriculture, and commerce, eventually becoming wealthy from his efforts.

Magic users knew him as a powerful wizard who'd been mostly interested in improving his own fortunes. Mylantis had been brutally efficient in stepping on anyone who got in his way in reaching that goal.

But people needed their heroes. And allowing them the fiction of his greatness was better than having them discover the horrible things his magic had done before he was conquered by the first Powers That Be over a century earlier. Fortunately, it was too long ago for humans to remember the battle in the very square where his statue stood. A battle

\

which had all but leveled the Enchanted of that time.

The monster stared at us through enormous, googly white and black eyes as crumbs fell to the ground from his wide maw.

"At least he doesn't have any teeth," I said.

Sebille stood, her hand glowing with unspent energy, and her expression nostalgic.

"What are we going to do?" I asked my two companions.

Grym grunted noncommittally.

Sebille shook her head. "I grew up with that show. Blue is kind and funny. All he wants is cookies. He's harmless."

Grym pointed to the unmoving forms in the center of the street, the wreckage of several cars. The stench of burning rubber and smoking oil threatened to overcome the sweet temptation of broken cookies. "Those people would probably disagree."

Fortunately, the people I could see in the street had started moving. They were alive. However, the monster spotted them when they moved and started to rise. "We need to draw him away from town," I said, carefully avoiding discussion about what would happen next. I was deathly afraid that taking out the blue monster would require my assistant to seek therapy, and that would, in turn, require the therapist to seek professional help once Sebille was done with him or her.

It was a nasty cycle I'd rather not initiate.

Grym reached for his gun and stopped, his expression bleak as he stared at the huge weapon.

Apparently, even he was unsure that he could do what needed to be done.

"We need to capture him alive," I told them both, pretending not to see the relief in both of their faces at my declaration. "It's the best way to find the artifact."

I had no idea if that was true, but it served the current purpose of not assassinating a favorite childhood character in front of the goddess and everybody.

I looked at Sebille. "Can you put your phasers on stun?"

The sprite chuckled, nodding.

She had her nostalgic television shows. I had mine.

The monster straightened with a roar and lifted its big, four-fingered blue hand. A giant cookie appeared in the hand and I relaxed, fully expecting the monster to stuff the cookie into its toothless maw, dropping crumbs all around as he always had in his television show.

Unfortunately, that didn't happen.

Whipping his hand like a championship frisbee thrower, the monster flung the giant confection right at us.

My eyes went wide.

Sebille yelped, energy thickening in her palms.

Grym raised his gun and shot the enormous treat heading our way.

A chunk of the cookie crumbled...hehehe...but it kept coming.

As it neared, I realized just how much trouble we were in. The thing was huge!

I screamed and dove sideways as Sebille popped away in a flash of fairy light. Grym dove after me.

We hit the ground a beat before the massive cookie slammed into the spot where we'd been, huge, hard chunks of it exploding away from the spot where it had landed and crashing painfully into us.

Agony swept through me as a piece of it, feeling like it was made of lead, slammed into my thigh and I screamed from the pain.

Grym had tried to cover me with his big body, but he'd only managed to cover my head and torso, leaving my legs and one arm vulnerable to the impact. But he was heavy, smotheringly heavy, and I was forced to stop screaming finally when my compressed chest ran out of air.

The detective grunted several times, his body juddering under what I could only assume was an assault from more chunks of concrete-like cookie. When the rain of heavy debris finally stopped falling, Grym shoved to his feet and took off running toward the monster.

Sebille was already there, hovering around the blue monster's head and firing green energy into his eyes and ears, probably hoping to annoy the monster until it ran away like the abominable at Croakies.

The monster was slow and clumsy, but what it lacked in finesse, it more than made up for in brute force.

At a full-out run, Grym leaped off the ground and wrapped himself around a tree at the monster's back, climbing rapidly until he reached head-height. Sensing Grym at its back, Blue tried to turn, but Sebille increased her efforts to distract and annoy and Grym launched himself at the enormous monster, landing on one sloping shoulder and grappling toward the thick neck for better purchase.

I stood there, my legs throbbing and my ego almost as battered. My friends were endangering themselves, and I was just standing there.

My magics weren't the defensive kind, and they were at their strongest when I was in Croakies. But my power had grown recently, and I hadn't really tested it against anything other than artifacts. Well, except for a brief jaunt in another dimension, which I don't think counted because magic worked differently in Plex.

I dithered for a long moment and then lost the luxury of dithering.

A small girl emerged from one of the crashed

cars, her steps uneven and her small form seemingly unharmed. Though she appeared confused. When she started walking, she headed straight for the enormous blue monster, a dazed smile on her little face.

Grym and Sebille were busy containing the monster.

I had to do something to save her.

I took off running, calling out to the little girl as I ran. But she didn't seem to hear me. She just kept walking. Despite Sebille's attempts to annoy and distract, and Grym's attempts to...do whatever he was doing up there...the monster's gaze slid slowly toward the little girl. The thing's wide lips curved, showing a mouth full of wide, square teeth in a grin that didn't look at all friendly or kind.

Without warning, the monster swung a hand at Sebille and sent her flying in a blur of green magic. Blue brushed at his shoulder and Grym fell, but he managed to grab onto some blue fur and hung on as the monster started toward the girl, a giant cookie forming in his four blue fingers.

"No!" I screamed, wishing some of the other people who stood around the perimeter, their mouths slack and eyes wide, would notice the little girl and move in. I was too far away, and I wasn't going to get to her in time.

Without conscious thought, I pulled my keeper's energy forward and fed some of it into my clumsy feet and sore legs. Suddenly I was moving fast, fast. Almost as fast as Sebille could fly.

The CM drew back his silly-looking hand, the grin widening as the googly eyes got a feral gleam. I saw his intent in the midst of that gleam.

And I was terrified I'd be too late.

I fed more power to my legs and pulled a thick ribbon of it to my hands.

"No!" I screamed again. "Stop!" I wasn't sure if I was yelling at the monster or the girl. But neither one listened. So I threw the energy filling my hands at the monster, and sped toward the little girl as fast as my sneakers could carry me.

The creature ducked the energy bolt I flung at it and gave a roar, taking off running right at me. The little girl didn't even turn her head as I ran up behind her, calling out for her to stop.

The ground shook, and glass splintered in nearby windows as the enormous monster thundered toward us, the googly eyes made angry and ominous by a thick slash of black brows that slanted inward at the corners.

Those hadn't been there before.

My heart pounded at the sight. He still held the cookie but he was clutching it in one hand, no longer looking as if he intended to fling it at the girl.

Instead, I was growing very afraid he intended to pound us into the ground with it. The teeth in the blue monster's mouth had turned sharp, pointed like a shark's teeth, and spittle dripped from between the snarling lips.

When I reached the girl, I placed a hand on her shoulder and tugged her around, looking into a pair of glazed green eyes. "You need to go over there," I told her, pointing toward the people standing on the sidelines. I caught the eye of a big man with short dark hair and some type of uniform on and he blinked, seeming to realize for the first time how much danger the girl was in.

"Help her!" I yelled, giving her a shove in his direction and praying he got her out of there in time.

I turned away, running in the opposite direction in the hopes the monster would follow *me* instead of the girl.

A dragonfly buzzed past, green-tinted magic sifting over me as the sprite burst into full size again and ran beside me.

The thunderous sound of the creature's footsteps was growing steadily nearer, so I knew my gamble had worked.

The blue monster was following me and Sebille instead of the girl.

I would have breathed a sigh of relief, but the really mean version of the blue monster was following *us*!

Sebille leaped up onto an overturned car and whipped around, energy thick in her palms.

I scrambled over the car and turned too. My gaze

found Grym, still riding the monster's shoulder. Somehow he'd managed to hold on. In the blink of an eye, the gargoyle's arm turned to rock from the elbow down. The detective used the rocky fist to punch the monster in the side of the head.

Blue skidded to a stop with a roar, one big hand swiping at Grym. The gargoyle was no longer there, he'd scrambled across the monster's back and was rearing back to put another hurt on the thing's other ear.

Sebille fired energy into the monster's face, the green magic an iridescent bolt that shot straight toward an oversized, googly eye.

I tugged power forward and sent as much as I could gather into the monster's chest, praying it would at least slow him down.

With a scream that was equal parts rage and pain, the enormous creature fell to his knees, crunching a fallen motorcycle and parts of two crashed cars beneath him. He launched the cookie he was holding as he fell, another one appearing almost immediately to replace it.

I ducked. Sebille threw herself behind the car and sent energy into the rock-hard treats as they sailed overhead, turning them into chunks of debris that hit the street behind us.

Grym punched the thing a few more times, hard enough to send its head slamming sideways, and then jumped from his shoulder and slid down his side to strike him in the kidneys.

If he even had kidneys. For all we knew, the monster was filled with frosting and chocolate chips.

But whatever he hit, Grym's attack seemed to have had an effect. And, when my magic finally slammed into him, the house-sized blue monster gave another roar, his body shimmering on the crumb and energy-laden atmosphere, and then disappeared on a whoosh of sugar-scented air.

Grym landed on his feet where the monster had been, panting from his efforts.

A small, white rectangle drifted downward and bounced against the ground with a soft plop.

Panting with adrenaline, I moved around the downed car and hurried over as Grym bent down to pluck the sheet of paper off the ground.

His eyes went wide, and he looked at me.

"What is it?" I asked.

He frowned, handing it to me. "I think this is yours."

I scanned the sheet of paper, Sebille reading over my shoulder.

A stunned moment later, I said, "It's not possible."

Sebille's long, freckled face was formed into a scowl. "There has to be some mistake."

It was the artifact wrangling order for a video of the show the blue monster was known for. I recognized it from the pile of orders we had back at Croakies.

And across the top of the order was a large, black stamp.

Canceled, by order of the Société of Dire Magic.

6

ALL UP IN MY BIDNETH!

"Find out where he's staying," I barked at Grym, beyond angry. Agent Rogers had been all up in my bidneth about everything that had happened over the last several months and then, when he'd already given me a hard time about that monster, I find out it was his own department that canceled the order to find and confiscate the artifact causing the monster problem in Enchanted.

Silence met my command, and I turned to find Grym staring at me with raised brows.

I took a deep breath. "Sorry. I'm beyond ticked at this point." I held the page up between us. "We've been running around, risking life and limb trying to stop this thing. People were badly hurt today because of it. And this cancelled order tells me the Société not only knew about the source of this mess, but now they appear to be trying to cover it up."

He nodded. "I feel your pain, Naida. But this stuff needs to be handled very carefully. These are powerful people who could make your life miserable."

"They already *have* made my life miserable," I grumbled. But I knew he was right.

"Why don't you let me handle this," Grym said. "You and Sebille focus on finding the artifact."

I stared at him a long moment, slowly realizing what he was telling me. "You want me to keep working this, despite the fact the order was canceled?"

Holding my gaze, Grym slowly crumpled the order into a tight little ball, holding it out to Sebille. Grinning meanly, Sebille touched the paper, engulfing it in green energy. The ball of magic hung on the air between us for a moment and then disappeared with a soft pop of sound. "What cancellation?" he asked, his expression carefully neutral.

I glanced at Sebille and she shrugged. "I didn't see anything."

Sighing, I nodded. "You have our backs on this?" I asked Grym.

He didn't hesitate. "I don't know what you're talking about. Why would I need to have your back?"

My frown made him soften. "But, just in general, you have my word that I'll always have your back."

I bit back the angry retort that leaped into my mind. He hadn't always had my back, which was why I'd been dealing with having the Société all up in my bidneth over the last few months. But, in fairness, the detective had barely known me when he'd submitted those first reports. He'd had no reason to take my side over the responsibilities of his job.

Still...

"Okay." I glanced at Sebille. "We'll focus our combined energies on this thing and try to close it down as fast as possible. Agreed?"

The sprite nodded. "First, I think we should go see my mother. She might have some insight into what we're dealing with."

I nodded. "See you later?" I asked Grym.

He reached out and touched my arm, smiling warmly. "Of course."

A warm, fuzzy feeling sifted through me. I had to tighten my lips to stop an answering smile. "Thanks," I said, my tone as neutral as possible.

I watched him leave and then turned to my assistant. "What do we have in the library that might be useful against this thing?"

Ultimately, we decided to talk to Queen Sindra first. Once we had a better idea what we were dealing with, we could hopefully decide how to combat any monsters we encountered.

The door into Lea's greenhouse was unlocked. We stepped inside, calling out as we entered.

The air sparkled with energy from the dragonfly-sized creatures buzzing from plant to plant. The Fae were sifting fairy magic over the plants to strengthen and enhance them.

I stood inside the door and inhaled deeply, closing my eyes to better enjoy the sweet scent of ripening fruit and blossoming flowers.

Lea was bent over an enormous rose bush, carefully pruning it while gathering vibrant red, yellow, and pink buds on long, thorny stalks. She placed the flowers into a shallow basket and smiled up at us. "Hello, Ladies! What a nice surprise. You're just in time for tea."

The thought was enticing. Like Sebille, Lea made an excellent cup of tea. My own attempts at tea-making pretty much resembled burnt dirt water that was so strong it made my taste buds curl into the fetal position.

"We need to talk to mother," Sebille said. "Is she here?"

Lea shook her head, climbing gracefully to her feet. My friend, the earth witch, was a softly rounded woman with shoulder-length light brown hair and a pretty turquoise gaze. She collected her basket, tucking a thick ribbon of wavy hair behind one delicate ear. "Sorry, Sebille. She's talking to the *Illusion City Council* about a place in the primordial forest."

Lea's pretty face tightened as she gave us the bad news. I was pretty sure Lea didn't want the Fae to leave her greenhouse.

"I thought they'd decided to stay?" I said, skimming Sebille a glance.

My assistant didn't look surprised. And she wouldn't meet my gaze. Both things that didn't bode well for Queen Sindra doing what Lea and I would both like her to do.

"I've tried to talk her out of it," Lea said, finally giving in to the frown dancing on the edge of her expression. "But, she insists she needs to have the conversation." Lea sighed, cocking a hip. "She thinks she's intruding in my space here."

"But we all told her we want them to stay." I stared at Sebille until she turned to me. When she finally did, I was surprised to see the hurt in her gaze. She wanted her mother to stay close by too. But I knew she'd never admit it. All she said was, "My brothers and sister live in the primordial forest. They've been putting pressure on her to come."

So that's what the problem was. "That's too bad. I love having her here, and it's safer than the forest," I said.

Lea nodded. "I told her that too."

We shared a moment of disappointed silence. But Lea had never been one to wallow. She forced a smile. "What did you want to ask her about? Maybe I can help?"

The question was almost a plea. I realized my friend would welcome having something to think about other than losing the company and magical green thumbs of her Fae guests.

I quickly explained to Lea what we were up against. She listened in silence until I was done, merely lifting a delicate brown eyebrow when I told her about the cancellation order.

Finally, she nodded toward the door. "Come on. I could use some tea. It sounds like you probably could too."

Hex appeared from among a dense bunch of herbs that had to be as tall as my arm was long and trotted after us into Lea's shop, *Herbal Remedies with Mystical Properties*.

Once inside the shop, Lea put her freshly cut rose buds into a plastic container of water inside a glass-fronted refrigeration unit, touched the water with a fingertip, turning it pale green, and closed the door. While she gathered tea things, we discussed mundane subjects like business and weather and our beloved cats. I told Lea I'd left my three little monsters in my apartment doing goddess knew what and she laughed, telling me I'd do well to pay better attention to them because they were fully capable of getting up to no good and dragging me into it with them.

She wasn't wrong.

Lea filled a pot of water and settled it onto an

old-fashioned stove, setting dainty, flower-patterned cups and saucers out for the three of us.

I watched as she filled a frog-shaped tea infuser with a variety of different loose teas and grinned at the frog, which had been a gift from me after we'd both gotten frogs.

My taste buds were already looking forward to whatever mixture she thought best suited the moment.

The sweet, floral scent of the tea tantalized my senses as she filled my cup several minutes later and I inhaled gratefully.

Lea dug a container of raw clover honey out of the tea cabinet and set it on the table, along with spoons. "Peach, sage, and sunflower for wisdom," she told us. "Passionflower and lavender for calm."

I added half a teaspoon of honey to the tea and stirred, tasting it with a sigh. "That's so delicious."

She settled herself into a chair at the small table and Hex jumped into her lap, curling into the soft fabric of Lea's usual long skirt and closing her eyes. A loud purr filled the air around us and I smiled, feeling right at home.

The shop was warm and the tea was soothing. Like Hex, I was sleepy. It wasn't long before I felt my own eyes starting to droop. I was aware of Lea and Sebille chatting easily as they sipped, so I let my eyes close and felt my muscles relax. Sometime later, Lea's voice roused me.

I jerked awake, my nerves buzzing, and looked back and forth between them. "Sorry. I guess the passionflower was too soothing."

Lea laughed. "You look tired." She glanced at Sebille. "You both do. You need rest."

"We can't," I said, sipping my tea. "You should see the pile of orders at Croakies. And now there's this monster artifact to find..." I let the sentence trail away, feeling suddenly overwhelmed.

Lea got up and returned to the cupboard where she kept her tea things. "I've been trying not to eat these, but I consider this an emergency."

Her back to us, she filled a small plate with something I couldn't see and returned to the table, setting it in front of us.

The rich, decadent scent of moist chocolate teased my senses.

Sebille's stomach growled loudly and she flushed.

I grinned. "Frosted brownies? It's a good thing Hobs isn't here."

Lea took a brownie and placed it on her napkin, tearing off a dainty bite and pressing it between her lips. "It's his fault I have these. I never even thought about eating brownies until he came around."

Sebille and I dug into our own brownies. I was decidedly less dainty about mine than Lea had been. I suddenly realized I'd missed both breakfast and lunch. No wonder I was nodding off.

"Okay," Lea said. "Let's talk about this monster problem."

I nodded, licking my fingertips. "The first one was an abominable-type ice monster. He showed up inside Croakies and coated the place with ice."

"Books were flying around too," Sebille said, her teeth brown with chocolate. "Do you think that's significant?"

"It could be," Lea said. "Winter Monster?"

"That's what we thought," I said, popping the last bite of my brownie into my mouth. I pointed to the plate and Lea nodded, pushing it close to me. I grabbed a second one, feeling the chocolate reviving me. "But then we met Mean Blue."

Frowning, Lea wiped her fingertips on a paper napkin. "You see, that's where I get confused. My first thought was that we were dealing with a Fiction-to-Reality artifact. Something that brought stories to life. But there's no story that I know of which has the blue monster attacking people."

"And more interesting. He changed even while we were dealing with him. He got furious-bird eyebrows, and his teeth sharpened," I said.

"He shouldn't have even had teeth," Sebille said, frowning.

Lea and I nodded.

Lea sipped her tea, her expression thoughtful. She said, "It's obviously some kind of transformational artifact. The artifact in play transforms something... thoughts, dreams, memories, books, or movies...into real-life versions of the object being transformed."

"What could do that?" I asked, running through my knowledge of the artifact library contents for something even close in purpose.

Lea shrugged. "You'd know that better than I would, Keeper." She grinned. "But I'd guess you're looking for something that makes the imagined real. And, since the two monsters were so different, it would be something that feeds on more than one source."

"Like a book or camera," Sebille suggested.

Lea thought about that for a moment. "A camera, maybe. But not a book, unless it's an anthology of different monsters."

"Maybe something more along the lines of a typewriter or a recorder," I offered.

"Typewriter, possibly," Lea agreed. "But a recorder is verbal or aural. I think we're probably looking for something visual."

"Then that leaves out a typewriter, doesn't it?"

"Not necessarily," Lea disagreed. "Words can paint a picture if they're written well."

I nodded. "True. It sounds like I need to do some research."

"I'd like to help," Lea said, repeating her offer. "I can create a tracking spell if you can give me an idea what I'm tracking and put me within a fifteen-block radius of it."

And that was the trick, wasn't it? But I didn't say it aloud. It wasn't Lea's job to find rogue artifacts. It was mine. I stood and gave Lea a one-armed hug. "Thanks for the tea and snack. And for helping us think this through. I'll get back to you when I know enough for that spell."

Lea nodded, looking thoughtful. "There is one other possibility for tracking this artifact." She seemed reluctant to even offer the thought she was apparently having.

"What's that?" I asked, half expecting her to change her mind about offering it.

She didn't. "If it's dark magic, we can use the cats." Lea ran her fingers along Hex's back, and the little cat purred louder, the sound sweet and hopeful against the darkness of Lea's words.

Hex and Wicked had been part of a litter of five cats, bred and trained to help dark witches perform black magic. It was something Lea and I hated to think about. Not because we thought it diminished the cats in any way. It hadn't been their fault they'd been used for ill. But it was a sad reminder of how horrible their early days had been. I reached out and scratched the little cat behind her ears. She looked so much like Mr. Wicked that I'd had an instant fondness for her when we'd met. I'd do almost anything to keep her safe, as I would Wicked, Slimy, and Hobs. Which meant, not putting any of them in a situation where they'd need to dabble in the dark magic they'd been created for.

"Hopefully, it won't come to that," I told my friend. I offered her a smile and Sebille and I left.

7

WE DON'T EAT THE SONGBIRDS AT CROAKIES

A moment later, as I stepped into Croakies, I learned just how wise my friend the earth witch was.

Not about using the cats for a black magic spell. Fortunately.

But about my three "monsters" getting up to trouble while I was gone.

Sebille threw open the door with her usual gentle touch, slamming it against the wall hard enough to make the glass rattle in the window. She stopped dead in her tracks just over the threshold. I slammed into her with an "umph" sound. "Sebille, use your brake lights if you're going to stop short," I groused.

She ignored me, staring in shock at the sight laid out before us. "Holy elastic belly band for the goddess's favorite girdle," the sprite said.

I peered around her, seeing what looked like snow all over the carpet, the books, the walls, and the three small creatures standing in the middle of the room.

Panic flared in my belly, twisting it tight. "The Winter Monster's been back," I murmured, horrified.

Sebille turned and rolled her eyes at me. "Look closer."

I stepped around her, casting a critical eye over the trio, starting with the hobgoblin. He was white from head to toe. His big blue eyes the only part of his little form that wasn't coated in white. When he blinked, the pale blue orbs briefly disappeared into the all-white terrain of his small round face.

Next to him was a cat-shaped form, similarly draped in unrelenting white, round orange eyes peering out at me through the snow-like covering. A white tail snapped the air unhappily behind him, and the hair along Wicked's spine was standing straight up in a dusty white salute.

Casting my gaze down, down, down to the floor, I glowered at the frog. "I'm guessing you're a rare white albino frog?" I asked the dusty white amphibian.

Slimy's white throat expanded and shrank, dust filtering down to the white-washed carpet. *It was the hobgoblin's idea*, Slimy said inside my brain. Since returning from Plex, a place where magic acted differently, Slimy's "conversation" had taken place strictly inside my head. Which had taken some getting used to after hearing him converse aloud the entire time we'd been in Plex.

I told him it was a stupid idea, sayeth the irritated frog.

Sebille snorted out a laugh.

"We were playing Winter Monster, Miss," Hobs said, his pale blue orbs widening earnestly as he tried to defend himself against the frog's accusation.

The cat was not a willing participant, Slimy went on. *Hobs dumped a whole bag of flour over him. Wicked's not happy.*

I fought a grin. "I'm surprised you let yourself be dipped in flour," I told the frog. "I mean, one false step into a puddle of hot grease and, viola! You're a French delicacy."

Sebille's snort of laughter burst into full-on giggling.

I joined in, despite the unholy mess they'd made of the store. "You're going to clean this up," I told Hobs.

His little shoulders drooped. "Yes, Miss."

I took pity on him. "Use Cinderella's wand. It will clean this up in no time."

Hobs grinned widely. "Yes, Miss!" He shot away, leaving a trail of white powder sifting on the air behind him, and slammed through the dividing door much as Sebille had the front. The little hobgoblin disappeared into the artifact stacks, where I had no doubt he knew the exact location of the wand in question.

The hobgoblin spent a lot of time clambering over the shelves back there. He probably had a better idea of each artifact's location than I did.

A happy Spring song trilled through the store, and I glanced to the top of the nearest bookshelves. Pretty yellow and blue songbirds lined the entire shelf, round black eyes staring down at us and heads cocking as they happily warbled.

Oh yeah, there's still that problem. I thought, sighing. I was starting to feel depressed by all the stuff I needed to fix. I hadn't made progress on any of it.

Without warning, one of the birds flew down from the shelves and swooped low, diving at Slimy and trying to peck his floury outer layer.

Ah! The frog shouted, hopping sideways with bulging black eyes. To be fair, Slimy's gaze always bulged. But it might have gotten even bulgier in that moment. If that was possible.

Wicked leaped at the bird and batted it from the sky, sending it rolling across the rug.

There was a gleam in my cat's eyes that was instantly alarming. "No, Wicked!"

He pounced...

Fortunately, the sprite was faster. She grabbed up the fallen songbird and held it against her chest, glaring down at my cat. "Back, you blackguard. We don't eat the songbirds at Croakies."

I snorted. "Those are seven words I never thought I'd hear."

Mr. Wicked held his own in a stare-off with the sprite for a few beats and then, with the whip of a dusty tail, turned around and stalked toward the door into the library.

He came running back a moment later, eyes even rounder than usual and tail standing up along his back. Hobs chased after him, swinging Cinderella's wand on his trail.

"Bibbity, Bobbity, Boo!" sang the hobgoblin.

A burst of sparkly stars emerged from the tip of the wand and shot after Wicked, quickly catching up. The magic flashed along his tail, over his back, and swamped his cute little gray head in a rainbow-covered starburst.

The energy lifted my cat right off the rug on an alarmed yowl and set him back down several feet away. Wicked took off running as if the hounds of Hades were nipping at his tail. He was gray again. But not happy about how he'd gotten that way. I was pretty sure we wouldn't be seeing him again for a while.

Hobs, however, was delirious with glee. Cackling happily, he pointed the wand at Slimy.

Oh, no, noooooo! The frog tried to hop away, but he wasn't nearly fast enough.

Like Wicked, Slimy was wrenched off the carpet by the happily sparkling stars, but Hobs must have put a little too much into his Bobbity or his Boo because Slimy did a quick somersault on the air and landed on his head with an alarmed croak.

Without further ado, Hobs turned the wand on himself. "Bibbity, Bobbity, Boo-ooooohhhhhh!!!"

Stars burst from the tip, larger and sparkly-er than before, and smacked into Hobs hard enough to send him shooting backward. He slammed through the open dividing door and disappeared from sight, the sizzle of the wand's cleansing magic splayed out like a jet-stream behind him. There was a crash as Hobs met some immovable object beyond the door.

Sebille, still clutching the songbird against her flat chest, ran toward the door with a worried expression.

I knew better. Rolling my eyes sprite-style, I reached down and flipped the frog back over, then stood back and waited, counting it out inside my head. *One, two, thr...*

"Again!"

I chuckled, shaking my head. All was as it should be at Croakies.

The exterior bookstore door slammed open. I spun around, energy spitting on my fingertips. I stared at the door, waiting for whoever had slammed it open to come through. *Nerves much*? you might ask. Yes, after everything that had happened, I was a little on the tense side.

Nothing came inside.

Amid fighting sounds, some random hissing, and flesh against flesh smacking, I watched the open door for several beats. Long enough for me to consider walking over to see what was going on outside.

Movement in the big window had my eyes widening as Detective Grym flew backward and smacked against a car parked at the curb in front of the store.

An alarm sliced into the usual afternoon sounds of people going about their business on the neighborhood streets.

The doorway darkened. A curved pair of fangs and a truly ugly face came through the door, followed closely by a disgusting pair of black, beady eyes, perched wide on a furry black head. Behind the larger two eyes in front were three more perched on either side of the head. Two hairy legs, bent and spindly, slipped through the opening on either side of the head, then two more, and two more. A thick heavy carapace, covered in the same black fur, somehow slid through the doorway with the legs. And finally, a bloated abdomen and two more sets of legs followed.

I shuddered with revulsion. I was staring at a black spider that stood as tall as me, eyes gleaming with hostile intent and fangs clanking aggressively together in front of a nightmare-inducing mouth.

I swallowed hard, feeling my guts twist with

dread.

"Goddess," Sebille murmured. "That's..."

Since she seemed at a loss for the appropriate word, I helped. "Hideous," I suppled.

Sebille yanked me back and threw up a shimmery wall of green energy just as the monster-sized spider shot forward with alarming speed, fangs snapping down where we'd been standing.

Sebille's magic barrier captured the thing's slimy fangs and held them as the spider yanked and writhed against it, sending streams of yellow liquid into the air and creating violent ripples in the barrier.

A massive form lumbered through the door. I tore my gaze reluctantly from the spider, feeling as if it would leap on us if I let my attention slip away, even for the space of a single heartbeat.

Grym had changed to his gargoyle form, a look of pure determination in his dark-caramel gaze. He punched the monster's carapace with an enormous, rocky fist.

The spider barely seemed to notice. It was pushing into the barrier, stretching it toward Sebille and me.

With a burst of green energy, Sebille popped into her sprite form and took to the air, flying over the barrier and sending magic streaming into the spider's face.

It stumbled back, making a knee-melting hissing

sound, and lifted up on its hind legs to throw a string of sticky webbing at Sebille.

She managed to dodge the first web, but the spider was fast. It sent three more streams of the stuff at Sebille's dodging form as her energy bolts tore into its carapace, sending green blood splashing into my carpet.

Ish!

One of the web strands found the sprite, wrapping her in a gummy, unbreakable embrace. She struggled against it but was unable to get even her hand free of the sticky substance. Fortunately, the webbing hadn't caught one of her hands and she tried firing energy at the spider as it started to reel her in. The spider simply tugged on the webbing, causing her energy to go dangerously awry, creating scorch marks on the carpet and even blasting into the barrier protecting me.

I watched in horror as Sebille was drawn toward the monster's disgusting face, knowing it would inject her with its poison and, at the very least, she'd be immobilized from it. And, at worst, it would kill her.

Grym pulled a gun from somewhere behind his back and screamed, "Down Naida!"

I realized why he'd been hesitant to use the weapon before. In the confined space of the store, bullets were just as likely to hit me as they were to hit the spider.

I dove to the ground, and he fired.

Two of the bullets hit the monster's abdomen, creating untidy holes that spewed green blood into the air.

Some of the nasty blood hit Grym and he jumped away, looking at the dripping green goo on his chest and grimacing. Then his gaze widened in horror.

I saw the moment the poison started to do its thing.

Grym stopped moving, his huge, blocky form going rigid like the rock his magical form resembled.

"Naida!" Sebille screamed. My gaze jerked away from Grym to discover that Sebille was only a couple of feet away from the monster's terrifying fangs.

Slimy yellow poison dripped from the massive teeth, and I worried that Sebille's softer form would assimilate it more quickly than Gryms and it would quickly prove fatal.

I couldn't let her be drawn any closer.

Realizing what I needed to do, I considered calling on Blackbeard's sword. But the sword came with baggage in the form of a mouthy parrot, and I didn't want to endanger SB by putting his cocky self in the path of the spider monster. (The initials were short for Sewer Beak, because the parrot had lived among pirates for too long and his language reflected it.)

Fortunately, there was another blade I could call.

I threw out my hand, thinking of the sword I'd brought back from Plex. The blade had magic. It was more than just a sword. But it would work just fine to hack a monster spider into bits.

With a soft hiss of displaced air, the hilt of the blade smacked into my palm and my fingers wrapped around it in a comfortable grip.

"Take down the barrier!" I screamed to Sebille.

Sebille hesitated a beat too long. The spider yanked her several inches closer, despite the frantic beating of her butterfly-like wings on the air.

"Sebille, do it!"

Her hand came out and a thin stream of green magic shot toward the barrier. For a moment nothing happened. The barrier held.

Sebille was yanked nearer, managing to wrench herself to a stop only inches from the poisonous fangs. She'd begun to make a terrified keening sound that turned my blood cold.

I hacked at the barrier with the sword, desperate to help.

When I'd just about given up on Sebille's weak infusion of magic working to break the barrier, the energy wall finally wobbled, stretched, and then disappeared with a pop.

The spider turned its head, fixing its main two eyes on me with sudden interest.

Sebille shot it on the side of its head, apparently scoring a hit on one of its secondary eyes because it reared up with a scream, mouth flexing and compressing like the slits in an old-fashioned coin purse. Thin streams of green blood shot out to coat the nearest wall.

I didn't wait for the monster to return its attention to me.

Using my keeper energy to power my strikes, I danced forward and sliced a hairy leg at the joint. The spider screamed again, forgetting Sebille and darting toward me.

I sliced a second leg at the joint and then leaped away as green blood shot in my direction.

The nasty stuff barely missed me. I tugged at my energy and leaped, hitting the monster's carapace just behind her head.

I reached out and slashed at the string holding Sebille.

The sword didn't even dent the stuff.

I threw everything I had into a second strike on the sticky string, but it stayed intact. The spider whipped around, sending Sebille flying through the air like a rock on the end of a string, and I recognized what the spider intended as Sebille circled my way.

If I didn't do something, the string keeping the sprite immobile would find me, wrapping around me before I could even lift the blade to stop it.

I threw the blade up in front of me, watching as a blood-tinted light fluttered along the edge, and the magic of the spider's webbing was repelled, disintegrating as it came within the blade's magical sphere.

Sebille sailed off on a shrill scream and I spun, finding a tender spot between the bug's rocky carapace and the nasty head. Without another moment's hesitation, I drove the blade deep into the soft tissue and leaped away as the monster reared into the air one last time, screaming in agony, and then collapsed to the ground so hard it shook the building when it landed.

I landed not far away from Grym and stood there, breaths heaving in and out of my chest. When I could breathe well enough to speak, I said, "Sebille, are you okay?"

Her only response was a long, drawn-out groan.

"I'll take that as a yes." I slid a look over Grym, wincing. He was painted in the slimy green blood of the spider monster, his form immobile except for his dark gaze, which focused on me with an, "I can't believe I'm standing here covered in goo expression."

I almost laughed. Once, I'd been covered in goo. That time it had been from a giant stink bug.

It had been worse than gross.

"I feel your pain, Grym." Yanking my phone from my pocket, I quickly dialed Lea. When she answered, I kept it brief. "What do you have to counteract giant spider monster goo?"

8

I'M UP FOR AN ADVENTURE

"I don't think we can ignore the fact that two of these things ended up here, at Croakies," Grym said. He sat across from Lea and me at the table, his cheeks pink from a good goo-generated scrubbing and his damp hair standing up in adorable tufts at the top of his head.

Sebille stood behind the sales counter, staring at the dead monster as if she expected it to get up and start spinning webs again.

"You didn't tell us how you and that..." I slid my gaze toward the downed spider. "...ended up here."

"I have no idea how the spider ended up here. I was just coming to give you a report on the blue monster incident and saw that thing standing on the sidewalk. My only thought was to get it gone before any of the humans on the street saw it. Fortunately, the sidewalks were empty."

What he didn't say, although he could have, was that most of the shop owners and residents on my street were supernormals. Seeing a supernormal spider wouldn't have sent them into a dither. Despite that, I was pretty sure that having a giant spider monster sidling down the street would still have been cause for alarm.

"It looked like it knew where it was going," Grym said. "It was testing the door with its pedipalp when I first saw it."

When Lea and I lifted our brows in question, he pointed toward the feeler-type things on either side of the spider's ugly head. "Those."

"So why would a giant spider monster want to come into Croakies?" Sebille asked, her gaze not leaving the dead spider.

My fingers found the warm leather of the Book of Pages on the table before me, wondering why the book was back in the bookstore. "And why did an ice monster come in here?" I asked. Twice, if my suspicions were correct. I couldn't help remembering slipping on a random area of ice in the artifact library before we even knew about the monsters.

"Maybe one of the artifacts we've retrieved recently is calling them," Sebille offered.

It was as good an explanation as any. Still, since I'd come fully into my Keeper magics, I'd discovered that I could read each artifact pretty well once they were located in my domain, a.k.a Croakies. And I was pretty sure I hadn't read any latent monster-calling magic in any of the new stuff. "Have you checked them all?" Grym asked.

Sebille and I shared a look and burst out laughing.

Lea smiled around her teacup.

"I guess I'm missing the joke," Grym said.

"We have a thirty-five-foot-long table in the back piled up to our eyebrows in recently captured rogue artifacts," I told him. "And the orders are still pouring in. We're averaging fifteen a day since coming back from Plex."

Grym whistled. "That's..." His voice trailed off. Apparently, he didn't have words for what that was.

I didn't either. "We're in the *smile and pile* stage right now. If things ever slow down...or if we run out of space to store them...we'll start cataloging and assigning spots in the archives for them. Until then, all I have are my initial reads on each artifact."

"And?" Grym asked.

"And, I haven't read anything having to do with monsters."

He nodded, sipping his tea.

"You said you came to tell us about the blue monster?" I nudged.

"Yeah. With the New Year's parade not all that far behind us, we managed to convince the mostly human department heads down at the precinct, the media, and the general population that he was a parade float which got away from its handlers and blew down the street, causing cars to crash."

"And they believed that?" Sebille asked.

Grym gave us a crooked smile. "Madeline Quilleran gave the human population a little nudge with a vibration spell she sent through radio and television."

"It helps to have a PTB living nearby," Lea said, shaking her head.

"It does," Grym agreed. He frowned. "I spoke to Rogers."

My antennas went up. "Oh yeah? What did he have to say for himself?"

"To be honest, I think he was just as surprised as we were about the order cancellation."

"I don't believe that for a minute," I said, crossing my arms over my chest. "He's lying because we caught him looking stupid."

Grym shrugged. "Maybe. But I'm a pretty good judge of people and I believed him. He promised me he'd look into it."

I shook my head, not buying it. "Well, whatever Rogers says or does, it doesn't change the fact that we need to find the cause of all this monster-making before another one hits the streets."

"I'd be okay with never seeing another one in Croakies too," Sebille grumbled.

"Yeah..." I looked around at the devastation. Green goo dripped down the walls and hardened into glossy puddles in the carpet. Strings of sticky webbing draped over the books on the shelves, coated the floor, and hung from doorframes and light fixtures. "It's gonna take a minute to clean this up."

Lea patted my hand. "I have some goo remover in the shop. And it might work on the webbing too."

"Thanks," I told her, dredging up a smile.

My phone rang, and I looked down at the number. It seemed familiar, though I didn't know who it might be. "Croakies Bookstore," I answered, standing and heading for the sales counter to grab my list of book orders.

"Ms. Griffith?"

I recognized the English accent and cringed. "Hello, Mr. Pudsnecker."

"Ms. Griffith, I do apologize for ending our conversation so abruptly last time. I sometimes let my ego get in the way of my good sense. Will you forgive me?"

I thought about it for a beat, considering just telling him I was too busy to talk. But, in the end, good manners prevailed. "No, you were right, Mr. Pudsnecker. You're a local author, and I would like to become familiar with your work."

"Excellent! You should have received a packet from me in the mail. Have you looked at it yet?"

I frowned, glancing toward the spot on the

counter where Sebille usually put any packages we received in the mail. "Not yet, no."

"That is strange," he said, sounding pouty.

Grym and Lea waved as they left. I waved back, my gaze sliding to the giantnormous, dead spider. I wouldn't be able to open the store again until we got rid of it.

I braced myself for another ego explosion and said, "Our mail service can sometimes be slow. I'm sure it will turn up." I knew I should have asked him what was in the package, but to be honest, I didn't really care. I had bigger problems to manage. "Thank you so much for checking in, Mr. Pudsnecker."

"Oh. Very well, then. You'll give me a ring after you've seen what I sent you?"

"Yes, of course. Have a great day." I hung up before he could restart the conversation.

"Who was that?" Sebille asked.

"Some guy who keeps calling me. He says he's a local author."

"What does he want?"

I shrugged. "We never quite get to that. We keep getting stuck on the fact that I've never heard of him before." I shook my head. "Never mind him. What are we going to do with that?" I pointed at the spider.

Sebille put her hands on her hips. "Do we have any disintegrating powder in the library?"

I quickly scanned my mental inventory for disintegrating powder and came up empty. "Nope."

"The shoe-eating magic vacuum?" Sebille suggested.

I grimaced. "It would probably try to eat the whole spider in one bite and explode, spraying goo all over the store."

The bell on the front door jangled. I panicked, realizing I needed to put the *Closed* sign up and lock the door.

Fortunately, it wasn't a human customer.

"Hey," said Rustin, looking pleased to see us.

I grinned. "Hey, yourself."

A rainbow flew through the door and shot toward Sebille. My crabby assistant exclaimed in glee, her iridescent green gaze going wide with pleasure. "Sadie!"

The little creature was a rare amalgamate dragon from the rainforests of Hawaii. The dragon's color shifted constantly, encompassing every color of the rainbow, and her pretty slanted eyes changed colors with her mood. They'd turned a happy aqua as she chittered excitedly at Sebille. The sprite had taken an immediate liking to Sadie when Maude Quilleran had brought her to us and, despite the fact that Maude's aunt Madeline had summoned Rustin and Sadie back to her lab the last time they'd been with us, Sebille had remained firmly attached.

So attached, in fact, that it was almost vomit-making watching her coo and fawn over the adorable little creature.

"You escaped Madeline again?" I asked my friend the ghost witch.

Rustin laughed. "With her blessing this time. Maude convinced her it was a good test of my new duality."

Rustin's soul-form had been cast out of his body by his evil Uncle Jacob Quilleran, and he'd been dumped into a frog. A Slimy frog to be exact. *My* Slimy. His aunt, who wasn't part of the evil side of the Quilleran witch family though she was suitably scary, and Rustin's cousin Maude, also not evil, had been trying to fix Rustin by giving him a dual nature. Like a shifter. The idea was that he'd spend part of his time as himself and part of his time as an animal of some kind.

I hadn't seen his animal yet. I wasn't sure if I wanted to. I didn't know if he'd still be my friend when he shifted, or if he'd be something scary I'd need to avoid.

I also wasn't entirely sure what Sadie's role was pertaining to Rustin's new duality, but she'd started out as a potential source for the animal half of his dual nature. That hadn't worked out. But maybe the two of them were still connected in some important way. I'd promised myself I'd question Maude about it when I had more time.

"That Maude's a smart girl," I told Rustin. He

nodded and I gave in to the urge to offer him a hug. "We were worried about you." I pulled back and looked at Sadie. "Both of you. You disappeared so fast last time."

We'd been in the early stages of figuring out how to get Slimy, Hobs, and Wicked back after they'd jumped into a dimensional wrinkle and Rustin and the little dragon had just *Poofed* away.

"Sorry about that. I really wanted to help you with the wrinkle."

I shook my head. "Not your fault. I'm just glad you're here." I grinned. "Where are you staying?"

Rustin skimmed Sebille a look and shoved his wire-rimmed glasses up his nose. "I'm um... across the street."

His discomfort told me exactly where he was staying. I looked at my assistant to see if she'd noticed.

She saw us both looking at her. "Don't look so guilty, you two. Devard told me he'd rented my old apartment." Her lips spread in a slow grin. "I'm glad he rented it to you."

Rustin flushed and smiled, clearly relieved. "He told me to tell you that you can visit me any time. But you're not allowed to turn any of his customers into slugs."

Sebille's old apartment had been above the vapery across the street. A situation that more than pleased the sprite since she loved mixing up her own vape liquids and hanging out with Devard's regulars.

The slug thing had been an unfortunate occurrence that Sebille blamed on imbibing a bit too well on her homemade magical vapes. I believed the vape had been the cause of her momentary lapse because I'd been on the wrong end of one of her mixtures once. Let's just say there'd been a crow, a tiny saddle, and a very large loss of self-esteem involved.

And the crow might have lost a couple of feathers, though I'm blaming him for that. He should have taken off the minute he saw me coming at him with that saddle.

Stupid bird.

"Madeline told me you have a monster problem," Rustin said with a grin.

I sighed. "You make it sound like we're being overrun by cockroaches."

He laughed. "You might be able to handle it the same way. Maybe Theo has a monster trap in his shop."

Theo Gargantu was our local giant. He owned a pawn shop named Enchanted Collateral, which was a very fancy name for a shop filled with secondhand junk. Theo would be deeply offended if he heard me call his treasures junk, but one man's junk was another man's collectible.

"It might make sense to chat with him anyway,"

Rustin continued. "Some of his relatives are monsters."

I started to laugh and then stopped, realizing he wasn't joking. "Really?"

The ghost witch nodded. "Giants have limited options for suitable mates. Sometimes they find... erm...love in strange places."

I glanced at Sebille and she shrugged. "It's worth a try. Maybe he's heard of someone with an artifact that makes monsters."

It was true. A lot of rogue artifacts made their way through Theo's shop. Though he tried to keep his client transactions confidential, with the right incentive he could usually be convinced to cooperate.

"Okay, let's go. I need to stop at the bakery for a couple dozen of those huge sugar cookies he likes." I jolted to a stop at the sight in front of me. The line of songbirds from the top of the bookshelf were settled onto the spider, pecking at its disgusting, furry body. "What are we going to do with that?"

Rustin grimaced. "I think it's already being taken care of."

My eyes widened as I realized what he was talking about. "Ew!"

Laughing, Rustin shrugged. "Birds eat bugs, Naida. It's nature's way."

I stepped around the disgusting tableau and

headed for the door. "We're going to need more birds."

A deep-throated yowl of greeting preceded my cat through the dividing door. Rustin bent down to accept Mr. Wicked's greeting with a sound of pleasure, scratching him between the ears. "Hey, buddy. It's nice to see you." Wicked jumped into Rustin's arms and rubbed his head under my friend's chin, purring loudly.

The sight brought tears to my eyes. "He missed you too."

Rustin sighed, closing his eyes for a beat in enjoyment. "It's good to be back."

A green, red, and white blur shot into the room. Hobs skidded to a stop in front of Rustin. Despite his abrupt and unruly entrance, the hobgoblin held out his hand like a gentleman, his spindly fingers moving as if they had a dozen joints each. "Hello."

Rustin took the offered hand and shook it. "Hobs. Nice scarf."

"Thanks, Mr. Rustin. It was a gift from Miss Naida at Christmas."

Sebille rolled her eyes. "He hasn't taken it off since. I'm pretty sure if he did it would stand in the middle of the room all by itself."

Hobs frowned over that idea, clearly not seeing how a standing scarf could be a thing.

I gave the scarf a gentle tug. "Ignore her, Hobs. I think you look very handsome in your scarf."

When he'd shown up at Croakies, he'd been wearing only a white tunic type thing. I'd since had a tiny pair of white pants made for him. He never took those off either, though I'd offered to have clothes in other colors made. Hobs was a man with definite ideas and inflexible standards.

"We're going to see Theo the giant," I told them. "Would you like to come?" I barely kept from grimacing when I asked the question. I couldn't help thinking how much trouble Hobs could get into at the giant's crowded shop. But the hobgoblin paled, vehemently shaking his head.

Too late, I remembered Hobs' one and only encounter with the giant.

Theo had brought us something to trap the hobgoblin when we'd first suspected his presence at Croakies. And he'd made it clear he expected me to dispose of the little creature once I'd caught him, likening hobgoblins to invasive rodents.

Apparently, Hobs hadn't forgotten. "No thank you, Miss. There's work to be done here."

As if the idea of Hobs doing any kind of "work" at Croakies didn't strike pure terror into my heart, I forced a smile. "Okay. Be good," I told him, perhaps a bit too emphatically.

"Yes, Miss."

Wicked gave Rustin one last purring rub and leaped out of his arms, He did a quick drive-by rub on my leg and bounced after Hobs without a backward glance.

I'm up for an adventure, said a disembodied voice. I looked around and located the frog sitting on the carpet between the two bookshelves in the first row.

I grabbed my coat from the hook near the tea things and tugged it on. Sebille donned her own heavy coat. Winter was still holding sway over Enchanted, and the weather outside had been as damp as it was chilly. I fully expected to be hit with snow any day.

Slimy hopped over, eyeing the fallen spider as if he was considering it for dinner. "Don't even think about it, frog. You'd never get it into your squishy gullet." I scooped him up and tucked him into my pocket so he'd be warm.

Fat-shaming does not become you, he responded as Sebille and Rustin chuckled.

"Remember that the next time you make a joke about the size of my butt," I said before remembering Rustin was standing there. My face turned to fire as he chuckled.

"Your butt is just fine," he told me. "Not...erm... that I'd noticed or anything." It was Rustin's turn to turn the color of flame.

"Well, at least you two match," Sebille said on an Olympic-level eye roll. "Now, can we stop discussing Naida's butt and go speak to the giant?"

9

ALL RAINBOWS AND PLURPIE DOGS

*A*s a giant, Theopolis Gargantu lived in an artifact. What this meant was that everything in his living space was "alive" in a magical sense. Which was both fun and dangerous because you never knew what to expect when you walked into one.

Like its owner, a giant's home artifact was generally not aggressive, unless it felt the need to protect itself. However, also like their owners the artifact tended to crave accumulations of "stuff". And that stuff was always in a state of flux.

Fairytales never seemed to point out that giants were creatures of change. They sought it out at every opportunity, creating it themselves if it didn't naturally occur in their lives.

The store area of Enchanting Collateral was filled with normal, mostly non-magic stuff. Despite everything you might have heard about giants, they aren't stupid. In fact, they're really very intelligent. They know how to do two things very well, gather "stuff" and guard their magic.

Owning a pawn shop was a perfect profession for a giant. Nothing gathered stuff like a pawn shop. And as a magical creature, Theo often had magical items come through the shop. For that reason, I sometimes came around asking after a certain artifact's location. But one thing was certain. If I didn't come around, Theo would never call me. He guarded every bit of magic he accrued like it was the most valuable item in the Universe.

To him, it probably was.

This protective attitude had recently come to include the woman standing next to him behind the counter. His employee Birte, who was a rare silver dragon. And also Theo's girlfriend. You'd think a giant and a dragon, both magical hoarders, would be too competitive to get along.

Usually they were. But somehow Theo and Birte had found common enough ground to fall in love.

The big man lifted his head when we came through the door and grinned, his wide mouth filled with slightly crooked white teeth that looked like enormous chicklets between his lips. Theo was seven feet tall if he was an inch and probably weighed over five hundred pounds. All muscle. He hurried around the counter and moved through the racks and piles of stuff with the agility of a dancer, his deep-set hazel eyes widening with pleasure. "Naida, keeper! What a nice surprise."

The giant enveloped me in a hug that smelled like sugar cookies and I fought panic as his bulky limbs squeezed me hard enough to make my eyes bulge. I patted him on the back in the universal, "I give" signal and he released me, offering Sebille a shy smile. Before Theo found his dragon love, I was pretty sure by the way he acted around Sebille that he'd had a giantnormous crush on her. It was probably guilt over those previous feelings that currently held him to a simple wave when greeting the sprite in front of Birte. He shook Rustin's hand. "Mr. Quilleran, welcome to my humble shop. It's nice to see you again."

"Thank you for allowing me to visit," Rustin said a bit formally. Something passed unspoken between the two men but I couldn't read it. There were always underlying tensions between magical factions that I was mostly too busy and too uninterested to pay attention to.

I waved at Birte. She gave me her characteristic scowl but lifted her hand in a half-hearted wave. "How's Kanish?" I asked Theo.

We'd brought a feral dragon back from our adventure in the Plex dimension and we'd planned on having her stay at Croakies until she learned to change into her human form. When that hadn't happened within a reasonable timeframe, we'd made the hard decision to allow Birte to teach and protect Kanish until the young dragon learned her way around her new world. I hadn't seen Kanish for several days, but I'd been getting regular, if brief and slightly caustic, texts from Birte about the dragon's progress. Her latest text had been even more brief than usual and had contained only the word, *Success* with several asterisks behind it. I wasn't sure what it meant and had been planning to stop by for a visit soon even before our present predicament made it a necessity.

Theo's big face took on a secretive look that worried me. But there was a glint in his eyes that took some of the worry away. "Would you like to see her?"

I didn't miss the fact that he hadn't answered my question, but nodded anyway.

He turned toward the door to his artifact and called out, "Kanish! Can you come here a moment, please?"

After a moment that seemed to stretch into hours, the door slowly opened and a tiny, elf-like creature with short, spiky blonde hair and large blue eyes stepped through. She slid her gaze over us and quick tension turned her slight frame to stone. Biting her lower lip between pretty white teeth, she finally said. "Hi Naida. Sebille."

My pocket jiggled and the frog's face popped out.

He fixed a bulging black gaze on the young woman and he said, "Ribbit!" In my head I heard the words behind the sound, *Kanish*!

The young girl smiled, her posture softening. "Mr. Slimy. How are you?"

I blinked, tugging the frog carefully from my pocket. Of course he'd recognize her on sight. The frog seemed to have an extra sense when it came to magic. "You made your change," I said stupidly, relief throbbing in my throat. I immediately felt bad for the relief. I didn't want her to think I had anything against her magical form. It was just that she'd wanted to fit in so badly. And that would have been more difficult if she hadn't been able to embrace her human form.

Kanish nodded enthusiastically, her rosebud mouth spreading in a genuine grin. "I did!"

I hurried forward, pulling her into a hug. "I'm so happy for you."

She nodded and reached for Slimy. "Can I?"

I handed him over. "He's all yours."

She giggled, kissing him on his upturned snout. "I've missed you so much," she told the frog.

I barely kept from rolling my eyes. "Clearly, she doesn't know you very well," I told the frog. My teasing aside, it warmed the cockles of my heart to see them reunited. They'd formed a friendship in the trenches of Plex, when Kanish had been badly wounded in battle, and it had only strengthened during Kanish's time at Croakies.

Sebille appeared beside me, Sadie tucked into her arms. "You look great," Sebille said, her green eyes even more shimmery than usual.

Amazement filled me at the sight of my assistant's unshed tears. She *did* have a heart. Who knew?

Kanish's gaze landed on the tiny dragon and she squealed happily. "You have an amalgamate dragon!" She reached out and touched the tiny rainbow's chest, setting off a spurt of happy chittering from Sadie.

"Her name is Sadie," Sebille said proudly.

Without warning, the little dragon lifted off Sebille's palm and took to the air, delighting everyone with her acrobatic flying skills.

That is, everyone but Birte, whose usual glower seemed to take on an even deeper and more glowery tone.

The tiny rainbow landed on Kanish's shoulder and continued to chitter happily, her small wings lifting and lowering in emphasis of whatever she said.

Kanish nodded and responded in what sounded like the same language the baby dragon was using. Sebille and I shared a shocked glance.

"You understand her?" Sebille asked.

"Oh yes. It's a different dialect than I'm used to,

of course. But we had a large population of amalgamates on my home dimension." She gave us a delighted glance. "Do you know they're very good luck. And they have a wide range of surprising magics. You're going to enjoy her very much." Kanish said. Then her smile turned flat. "Just don't, you know, try to hurt her ever. They're not very kind to those who try."

Good to know. Not that we'd ever try to hurt her. "So she could defend herself if she needed to?"

"Oh yes. Probably better than you could. They're really very interesting creatures."

"But she's just a baby," Sebille objected, clearly not liking the idea that Sadie could take care of herself.

Kanish's response was a soft giggle. "Baby? Not hardly. I'd guess that Sadie was close to five hundred years old. Maybe even twice that, here. On my home dimension their lives are very difficult and the aging process is more pronounced. But here in this magical place you call Earth, I'm certain Sadie's life has been all rainbows and plurpie dogs."

I didn't correct her on the *plurpie* thing because I didn't want to embarrass her. Plus, for all I knew plurpie dogs might be a thing on her home dimension. "Well, that is interesting." I gave Sebille a comforting look. My assistant looked embarrassed at the knowledge that she'd been talking baby talk to a creature who was older than she was.

"She's still a juvenile though, liable to get into some trouble. So it would be wise to keep a close eye on her." Kanish grinned mischievously. "Especially around Hobs. He's likely to teach her some tricks."

Sebille looked slightly appeased. "Can you teach me her language?"

"I'd be happy to. If you'll bring her with you when you come so I can see her."

"It's a deal," Sebille said, grinning back.

Rustin stepped up behind us. "Hello," he said, giving Kanish a slight bow. "I'm Rustin."

Kanish returned the bow, her expression solemn. "It is a pleasure, good sir."

I figured the formality of her greeting must be something from her own dimension.

"What is it I can do for you today, Naida keeper?"

I looked at Theo, whose demeanor had turned all business. "We're being plagued by random monsters and we believe an artifact is causing it. Have you heard of anything like that?" I asked, carefully choosing my words so as not to in any way accuse him of harboring such a thing.

He held my gaze, his own sincere when he said, "I have not heard of a monster-creating artifact."

The way he said it, so carefully specific, warned me he might be withholding information from me. "Have you heard of an artifact that's in any way associated with monsters?"

His deep-set gaze skimmed away from me.

"There might be something. But it's very loosely related. Probably not what you're looking for at all."

"We'd like to take a look," Rustin said. "If you don't mind."

Theo didn't sigh, but it was a close thing. He jerked his head toward his home artifact. "I'll have to find it."

Ugh! I thought.

Sebille and I shared a glance. The sprite rolled her eyes.

We were going to be there a while.

I tried not to grin at Rustin. The ghost witch was perched on top of a chair seat, slightly crouched, with hands out to his sides and gaze constantly sliding around the space.

He had a giant knot on his temple, and his previously tidy jeans and white button-down shirt were rumpled and covered in dust.

I didn't think it had been the flying bottles, which had rushed across the room to greet him and clocked him in the head that put him on the defensive. I was pretty sure it was the California king-sized bed that had rushed him, hitting him behind the knees and then pummeling him with pillows until he couldn't breathe that had put that twitchy look in his gaze.

Unashamed, Sebille and I had taken full advantage of his pummeling distraction to make it across the room without being attacked by Theo's over-friendly furniture.

Still, I'd suffered a blow to one knee from a harmless looking stool embroidered with kittens and puppies. And Sebille was still picking pencils out of her long, fire-red braids.

The sprite and I were sitting on top of Theo's enormous desk. It seemed to be a safe zone of some kind because once we threw ourselves on top, the well-meaning artifact furnishings ignored us, turning their painful love on Rustin.

The ghost witch eyed us with jealousy, no doubt because we were relaxed and happy while he feared for his life at every moment. "Scoot over and make room for me," he said, dodging sideways as a small painting flew at his face.

"Not a chance. That lamp over there has its eye on you. If you head this way, it might come after you," I said as Sebille tittered happily.

"Come on!" Rustin whined. "I thought you were my friends."

"Stop whining, Rustin," Sebille said, examining her nails, which didn't bear examining since they were battered and torn. "It's so unattractive in a man."

Rustin yelped as a thick, leather-bound book

slammed into his belly. "I'll give you unattractive," he wheezed.

Across the room, stuff was flying into the air above Theo's bent form. He was muttering to himself as he searched through the endless piles, stacks, trails, and columns of stuff.

I glanced at my watch. We'd been there for over an hour. It was time to feed Wicked and Slimy, and I was pretty sure Hobs would start gnawing on my chocolate-scented candle if I didn't feed him something dark, sweet, and gooey pretty soon.

That gave me a terrible thought. I turned wide eyes to Sebille. "What if Hobs decides to try baking again?"

She snorted out a laugh. "I'm pretty sure he overloaded the wand last time, so I don't think he'll be able to use it again."

I sighed, "It looks like we're going to have more songbirds." My shoulders slumped with despair.

"Look on the bright side," Sebille said. "At least the spider will disappear faster."

I gagged, covering my mouth to hold it in.

Sebille snorted happily.

"Eureka!" Theo turned with excitement and held up an old wooden clock with carved wooden figurines on the front. As he held it up, a small figurine slid out through a rounded wood door and it chimed the hour, repeating the action five more times before it stopped. I glanced at my phone. Six o'clock. Perfect time. "Is that it?" I asked the giant.

He nodded. "An original Grimm clock. From the fairytale brothers."

I felt my eyes go wide. "You had *the* original Brothers Grimm clock buried in a pile on your floor?"

Theo tenderly caressed the wood. "Held in the gentle embrace of my loving home. Besides, it's one of six clocks they built. Not many historians know the Grimm brothers were talented clockmakers. They were much better known for their dark fairy tales." He held it up in one oversized palm. "This particular clock is entitled, *Dance of the Monsters*."

Rustin forgot his fear and leaned forward, his expression rapt. "I've heard of that clock. It's really a valuable artifact." He glanced my way. "I'm surprised you don't have an order for that, Naida."

I shook my head. "There could be one in the pile. It's growing every minute. I have no idea what all's in there."

Rustin opened his mouth to respond. He never got the chance. A roller-skate flew into the air behind Theo, dodged around the giant's head, and shot toward Rustin, hitting him in the chest.

Rustin grunted in pain and started to topple backward, arms pinwheeling. He lost the battle for balance a beat later and crashed to the floor, his arms clutching the roller-skate like an ardent lover.

10

THAT'S THREE DAYS IN STOMACH YEARS

I stared at the tiny monster inside the rounded door. It looked exactly like the Winter Monster that had been at Croakies. The figurine stared back at me through eyes that seemed to glow with malevolence. I let the door close and looked the clock over, seeing none of the other monsters in the figurines on the clock. There was a small child, kneeling beside a patch of some kind of flowers. The only spider was crawling over the ground nearby, its nasty eyes red and its mouth open wide, fangs appearing to be dripping with venom.

But it was not monster-sized. Bigger than normal, yes. But not as big as the one lying dead on the floor at Croakies.

I glanced at Rustin, who was holding an ice pack in each hand. One was pressed on the knot at his temple and one against the bump on his sternum, a few inches below his chin, which, I noticed, had a new dent in it.

I couldn't wait for Rustin and Grym to compare notes. When I'd brought Grym to Theo's, he hadn't fared much better.

"This has to be it, right?"

Rustin narrowed his gaze on the clock. "We can put it in the toxic magic room for a couple of days and see if any more monsters pop up."

Despite his suggestion, I got the sense that Rustin didn't believe the clock was our culprit. "You're not buying it though," I said.

He hesitated only a moment. "I'm just not sure. Like you said, there's only one monster on this thing." He pointed to the carvings covering the surface of the clock. "Those are of witches and children and feral animals. No monsters as we know them. Or, for that matter, as the Grimms with their phenomenal imaginations knew them."

"I doubt even the Grimms could have conjured up a blue monster," Sebille said, grinning.

Rustin snorted out a laugh. "You have a point."

"Maybe the magic takes its own creative license," I offered.

"It could," he agreed. But I still didn't get the feeling he was sold on the clock as our culprit.

"What?" I asked.

"I don't know. It just...doesn't feel malevolent," Rustin said finally.

He was right. It didn't.

Theo finished up with a customer and came over. "You know I can't give that to you without an order, Keeper."

I lifted my brows at his distancing of our friendship though use of only my title. "I see how you are."

He shrugged. "As Rustin said, it's valuable."

"I'm just going to put it in the toxic magic vault for a couple of days. If there's no order to bring it in, I'll give it back to you."

Theo settled a shrewd look on me. "You'll have to pay to take it out of the store."

Sebille put a hand on his broad shoulder, her arm barely long enough to reach that high. He looked down at her, growing instantly pale. "You know, Theo, Birte really likes Kanish. Being with another dragon makes her happy. It would be a shame if we had to ask Kanish to come back to Croakies..." She let the threat sift into the ether for him to assimilate.

It didn't take long. I hadn't believed he could get any paler. Somehow he did. Finally, he turned to me. "I'll need you to sign an agreement that you'll return the clock if no order turns up within three days."

"A week," Rustin bargained.

Theo thought about it for a long moment. "Five days. That's my final offer."

Sebille patted his shoulder and turned away. "Kanish?" she called out.

"Okay, okay," he glowered at the ruthless sprite. I was pretty sure any lasting dregs of his crush he'd been holding onto had just been extinguished. "One week. Seven days. And then you return it."

"If it's not our rogue artifact," I clarified. "And if I don't have an order for it."

He expelled air in an unhappy gust. "Deal. I'll go draw up the paperwork."

W e didn't even make it back to Croakies. My cell rang as we were driving away from Theo's. It was Grym. "There's trouble at *Vaped Delights*. I need you here yesterday. Bring Sebille. She might need to talk Devard down off the ledge."

"We'll be there in five minutes." I hung up, weariness bearing down on me at the thought of dealing with yet another problem. I turned to Sebille in the passenger seat of my little bug. Rustin was scrunched up in the tiny back seat. "That was Grym. He needs us at Vaped Delights." I fixed a look on Sebille. "He needs you to, I'm quoting, 'talk Devard down off the ledge'."

She flinched. "I'm not sure I'm the right person to..." She stopped speaking mid-sentence, her long face going white. "Naga."

All the blood left my face and I saw stars as I

realized what she was telling me. "*Snapping serpent sphincter,*" I murmured.

"What's going on?" Rustin asked, sitting forward to peer at us between the front seats.

"Devard's magical form is a Naga," I said, feeling as if I might throw up. I looked up and caught Rustin's blue gaze in the rearview mirror. "An ancient snake *monster.*"

"Oh," Rustin said. "Oh, goddess! That's not good."

"No, it isn't," I agreed. We not only had another monster, but it was one of our friends. We couldn't just kill it as we had the spider monster.

And the Naga was particularly terrifying and hard to control. Even Devard had trouble controlling the thing, and he'd presumably lived with it all his life.

"It didn't sound like the Naga had won yet," I told my friends. "Grym was hoping Sebille could help Devard stay in control." I glanced at my assistant.

She looked a little green.

That didn't give me much hope that we could head the monster off at the pass. And if it came down to battling the ancient monster, we were all going to become snake kibble.

I wasn't going down without a fight. I fully intended to make like a throwing star on my way down the thing's long, long throat.

I parked in front of Croakies and Sebille jumped out. "I have to get something from inside. Tell Grym I'll be right there." She ran off before I could respond, and I had to bite back a swear. Rustin dug his way out of my tiny back seat and stood, groaning. "I'd forgotten how much work it was hanging out with you."

I couldn't help it, I laughed. "Admit it, you were bored at Madeline's."

He shook his head, but I thought I saw a smile twitching on his lips. "What are the odds the sprite's heading for the Canadian border right now?"

"Zero."

He looked surprised and a little relieved.

"She's much more likely to head south to Mexico. It's just too cold for the sprite in Canada."

Rustin blew out a breath. "I really hate you right now."

I pinched his cheek, taking care not to bump the dragon-egg-sized knot on his temple. It had turned nearly black and stuck straight out from his head like a horn. "That looks like it hurts," I said by way of showing compassion. I wasn't my assistant with zero compassion. No, I wasn't.

"Yeah. It hurts a lot."

"Can I touch it?"

Rustin smacked my hand, barking out a laugh.

"Derf. Let's go see if we can wrangle us a snake, pardner."

"I was really hoping somebody else could do the wrangling. I'm too tired to wrangle. And it's been days since I've had anything to eat."

He threw an arm around my shoulders and led me across the street. "So, I guess those three tacos you ate on the way to Theos two hours ago didn't count?"

"You said it yourself. Two hours, Rustin. That's three days in stomach years."

We dodged around the cadre of police cars in the street, lights flashing and, in one case at least, doors standing open as if the cops driving them had flung the patrol car into *Park* and leaped into action.

Drama mama's. The street looked calm. There weren't even any gawkers yet. And I didn't hear any blood-curdling screams that told me the snake was preparing a nice appetizer for its Naida entrée.

The front of the building exploded outward, raining glass, drywall and...tail...at Rustin and me.

We leaped sideways, each of us going a different direction, as the enormous scaly protuberance swung wildly from side to side, ripping the open door of the nearest cruiser right off the frame and flinging it into another car.

I hit the curb when I landed, the rounded concrete compressing my hip bones with an audible crunch that promised excruciating pain once the adrenaline eased away. I rolled to a spot beneath the police car nearby and watched in horror as the snake's thick tail swept an entire car away and threw it onto its roof to skid ten yards down the street.

Rustin was back onto his feet and running my way. He leaped off the sidewalk, hitting the asphalt a few feet away from me and rolling to a spot behind the car.

Not that a little thing like a four-thousand-pound police vehicle would keep him safe. The car down the block, which was still wobbling on it back like a turtle, was proof of that.

"Okay, this is bad," Rustin said. "How do we stop this thing?"

"It's Devard," I said, near tears. "We can't kill him. Even if we knew how. Devard wouldn't have wanted this. It's not his fault, Rustin."

The ghost witch shook his head. "We don't have a lot of choices here, Naida. That thing's beyond deadly. Not to mention, nobody's going to believe the Naga is a parade float gone awry. Madeline Quilleran doesn't have enough magic to make this look right to the human public."

I knew he was right. But I had to think of some way to stop the Naga without compromising Enchanted.

A long, drawn-out scream of pain split the air and gunfire exploded inside the building. The moment of indecision had just passed. I turned to

Rustin. "Go to that building there and find a woman named Rhonda."

"Rhonda who?"

I realized with a start that I'd never gotten her last name. Or if I had, I couldn't remember it. "I don't know. Just stand in the hallway and yell for Rhonda. Tell her to stick her head out the nearest window and scream."

I started toward the vapery, and Rustin grabbed my arm. "You want me to recruit somebody to scream at this thing? I'm pretty sure the guy the snake's eating will do enough screaming to loosen our bowels."

I grimaced at the visual. "She's a Banshee. The snake will freeze when she screams. It worked before." I took off running before he could stop me. Heading toward the alley between the two buildings, I found a big rock and threw it at the nearest window. Then I climbed the fire escape and broke a couple more windows for insurance.

I wanted to make sure the snake didn't miss the Banshee's scream.

I stuck my head inside and saw a hallway. Stepping carefully through the window to avoid the jagged edges of glass I didn't quite clear away from the frame, I hit the carpet at a run and headed toward the sounds of fighting.

At the end of the hall was an elevator and a set of stairs.

No way did I want to ride an elevator down without knowing what I'd be looking at when the doors came open. I hit the stairs and descended them at as close to a run as I could, stopping at each level to peer through the fire glass. I didn't see anything until I hit the first floor.

All I saw there was a wide band of dark blue. When it moved, I realized I was looking at the back of a cop in uniform.

I knocked on the door and waved when he turned. He glared at me. "Get out of this building!"

"Detective Grym called me. I'm Naida Griffith."

Recognition lit the man's gaze and he stepped away from the door, pulling it open. "I still think you should run. This thing's crazy mad. I haven't seen teeth like that since I visited gramma in the woods wearing my red cape."

I snickered and he gave me a tight smile. "We have one cop down, and this thing's determined to take more of us."

I nodded, stepping around him. "Where's Grym?"

He pointed toward the main room, which was almost completely blocked from view by the massive coil of the Naga.

Enraged hissing sounds filled the air as I drew near. The smell of too much reptile made my nostrils twitch. At the end of the hall, I pressed myself against the wall and looked around for Grym.

He was in his gargoyle form, standing in front of two men who were hunkered down behind the shattered bar, their gazes glassy with fear.

Humans.

Just flippin' awesome.

Grym was brandishing the top of one of the red vinyl swivel stools that used to range along the front of the bar, using it to keep the snake from getting hold of the men he was protecting. I looked up at the sound of wings throbbing on the air and almost screamed at the sight of the demon diving at the snake, claws extended to swipe at the monster's snout on a fly by.

I realized a beat later that the demon must be a cop too.

Grym worked with a small group of Enchanted cops who knew about supernormals. It had never occurred to me that they might have magical forms themselves. I had no idea why I wouldn't assume that. After all, I'd known that Grym had another form.

The snake suddenly swung around, its hostile slanted gaze finding me. The thing's enormous head snapped upward in surprise. It didn't stay that way for long. Before I could say *blithering bat boogers*, the enormous mouth opened and the arm-length fangs were snapping downward.

A dragonfly-sized form appeared in front of me, butterfly wings beating the air hard as the tiny sprite blew a mist bathed in green energy toward the snake's eyes.

I screamed her name, certain she was about to become a small plate for the hungry snake, but Sebille held her ground, continuing to blow the mist from what I recognized as a tiny vape cigarette into the snake's ugly face.

I watched in surprise as the monster stilled, its eyes turning glassy and its movements languid as it wobbled on its coil like a drunk.

"Naida!" I turned toward the busted front window. Rustin stood on the glass-covered sidewalk. "She's about to let loose."

I nodded. "Cover your ears," I screamed to the police surrounding the snake. "Incoming Banshee scream."

Sebille blew one last blast of mist toward the monster and then flew away, I backed toward the hallway and joined the sprite and several cops in the elevator just as the doors started to close.

With three inches of space between the closing doors, someone stuck a hand into the space to stop it.

Then the scream hit.

I slammed my hands over my ears. But I knew it wouldn't be enough to completely stop the magic.

Blades of sound sliced through the room. Ripping the fragile flesh inside my ears to pulp.

Each bloated note swelled with unique power,

cutting deep. The scream boiled inside my head, tearing holes in my brain like a thousand tiny needles. Unrelenting pressure made my skull feel like it would explode.

I was vaguely aware of screaming. I didn't know if it was mine or one of the others inside the elevator with me. But my throat was raw so I was pretty sure my screams had joined the mix.

After a moment, the Banshee's scream dulled to a deafening throb, booming, booming, booming until I was pretty sure my brain was mush.

As it had the last time I'd been too close to a Banshee's scream, warm blood dripped from my nose and ears.

In the blink of an eye, the throbbing softened into a low, rhythmic hum and started to ease away. My mind felt numb. My body felt as if it had gained a hundred pounds. It was suddenly all I could do to blink. I tried to shift my legs, and it was like moving through quicksand. I had to fight to get even one hand to move.

But it did move. And, after a beat, so did my legs. I pulled air into my lungs and thanked the goddess I'd survived relatively unscathed.

Looking around the elevator, I met the gaze of the cop I'd spoken to when I'd arrived. He had blood running from his ears and nose but seemed other-wise unhurt. Sebille was crumpled on the floor in one corner, hands and wings covering her ears. I hurried over, touching her to see if she was awake. She groaned softly, her wings fluttering.

She was all right.

Not everyone had been so lucky. The cop who'd stopped the elevator doors was standing like a statue, half shifted into something that looked like it might be a wolf if it had shifted all the way. Charcoal gray fur covered bent legs with paws on the ends and painted his body up to about mid-chest. He was fully human from that point up, including having fur-free human arms and hands.

We pressed the button to open the doors and stepped around the frozen cop. I was relieved to see that the Naga had succumbed to the scream as he had before. Grym was talking quietly to one of his cops. The demon, I guessed, since the black skin and horns were gone, along with the wings, but the man's eyes when they focused on me still held a feral red light.

The two humans were frozen in place, drying rivulets of blood painting their pale cheeks.

A young female cop bent over them, her fingers creating a golden web on the air and her lips moving in a quiet chant.

A witch.

I nodded toward the two men and the witch. "She's spelling them to forget?"

The detective nodded, running a blocky hand over his rock-like face. "But we need to get this thing contained or we're going to be spelling a lot more humans."

"And burying a lot more," the demon cop growled out in a gravelly voice.

I looked at Sebille, whose face was tight with pain. She was back to her human size. "Will Devard get control of this if we give him time?" I asked the sprite.

She nodded. "We can help him along with herbal mists and things, but yes." She eyed the problem. "You're thinking the shrinking box?"

We'd used it once before to contain a dangerous monster. "Yeah." I lifted a hand and threw out my keeper magics, calling the box to me. When it came whistling through the broken front window, I caught it and handed it to Sebille. "You'll do the honors?"

She nodded, a strange hesitation in her movements as she took the box.

"What is it?" I asked.

Rather than answer, she held the box up so I could look through the door. I peered inside, my gaze going wide. "Ah. That's where you've been living all this time." Sebille and I had tried to share my apartment when Devard had first thrown her out of hers but it had been a dismal failure. Then, one day, she'd just up and moved out. I'd never been able to see where she went at night when she was done working and she'd worked hard to make sure I couldn't.

"I know it's against the rules to live in an artifact, but it seemed like the perfect solution."

And it had been. I thought about the problem for a moment. "Get your stuff out of there for now. We'll work something out."

She nodded, looking sad.

Finding Sebille better accommodations was a problem for another day. We couldn't get into it at that moment.

Not when I finally had a thought as to what might be going on with the monsters.

11

PLEASE CALL ME ARCHIBALD

*T*he spider was mostly gone by the time we got back to Croakies. It was little more than a gooey stain on the carpet.

My cat was draped over the windowsill of the big front window. He meowed when he saw me, his tail waving lazily below the sill, but he didn't jump down to greet us. He was no doubt enthralled by all the comings and goings across the street.

What's happening out there? The frog asked. *I can't see.*

I looked down to find him squatting, green and squishy at my feet. His bulgy black gaze fixed on me with earnest curiosity. I scooped him up and placed him on the wide marble sill next to Wicked. "Just don't hop off this windowsill," I told him. "Let me know when you're ready to get down."

Slimy hopped over and wedged himself against

Wicked's warm body. My cat lowered his nose to gently nudge his green best friend in greeting. I smiled wearily. It had been an exhausting day and it was good to be home.

Unfortunately, there were at least a hundred songbirds in the bookstore, sitting in tidy rows at the top of the shelves, throats throbbing on a constant stream of song.

I looked at the hobgoblin, who stood near the spider with a grin on his face and that blithering birdbrain of a magical hand vac clutched in his spidery fingers. "I cleaned it up, Miss," Hobs said, looking so pleased with himself I didn't have it in me to scold him for all the birds.

"Well, at least you won't need to buy birdseed any time soon," Sebille offered.

I nodded. "They look pretty fat and happy up there."

A pretty blue and yellow songbird fluttered down from the shelf and landed on Hobs' head, breaking into a Spring-worthy melody that inspired the others to redouble their efforts. The entire store throbbed in a chorus of happy bird ballads.

Sebille groaned. "All this sap-happiness is giving me a headache. I'm going to go put this stuff away." She headed toward the dividing door with her magically miniaturized possessions in a small box, her feet dragging with unhappiness.

Hobs took off running after her, slamming the dividing door behind him.

I was so distracted by the birds that it took me a minute to realize what she'd said. Sebille was going to put all her stuff in my apartment again.

Horror slicing a track through my belly, I started after her. There had to be another solution to her housing issue.

There just had to be.

I couldn't stand even one night of falling over her unending collection of furniture, losing out to her on the TV remote, or listening to her whistling snore all night long while sleep evaded me.

Unfortunately, before I could stop her, my cell phone rang. I looked down to a number that was becoming all too familiar. I really gave some thought to not answering. But something inside wouldn't let me do it.

Apparently, I was one of those people who'd stand, riveted, as two trains headed right at each other at breakneck speed.

"Croakies Bookstore."

"Ms. Griffith. How are you? Did you receive my package yet?"

His question was the final straw on my woefully overburdened camel's back. It was the electrical shock on my last, panting nerve. The final shoe dropping. The last ballad in my much-panned musical. The... Okay, you get it. It was just all I could take. "Mr. Pudsnecker..."

"Please, now that we're becoming friends, call me Archibald."

I'd rather call an Uber Eats and eat egg rolls in bed, under the covers, with my latest paranormal romance clutched in my greasy fingers. "Arch-i-bald," I stuttered out. "I'm in the middle of a bit of a crisis. I haven't even had time to eat. Why don't I give you a call when things calm down, and we can talk about you maybe doing a book signing here at Croakies..." I hoped he'd snatch at that little dangling carrot and agree to back off for a bit.

The exterior door opened, setting off the soft jangle of the warning bell hanging from the top. The man standing there had a cell phone to his ear and a happy light in his blue eyes.

He smiled, pointed to the phone at his ear, and said, "Too late. I'm already here."

Shock had me going perfectly still, the cell pressed against my ear.

Pudsnecker stepped all the way into the shop and hit *End* on his call to me, sliding his phone into the pocket of his tweed coat.

His gaze slid around the store, brightening when he spotted the birds and narrowing at the gooey remains of the spider monster. "Looks like you've had some sort of industrial accident," he said in his precise, English tones. Despite the cultured tone in his voice, there was humor throbbing in his voice.

I was surprised by that. I would have expected horror or disgust. The spider remains were pretty disgusting.

I gave a breathy chuckle. "Yeah. Ha."

Pudsnecker jerked his head, covered in soft brown curls that ran to gray at his temples, toward the mess of police cars across the street. "What's happening over there?"

Nothing much. Just an ancient snake monster attack that was thwarted by a demon, a gargoyle, and a banshee's scream.

That sounded like a bad joke. A demon, a gargoyle and a banshee walk into a bar...

"Robbery, I think..." I hated to lie, but I couldn't very well tell the human standing before me the truth.

He pursed his lips, nodding. "I wasn't aware that Naga were thieves." He laughed. "For that matter, I didn't realize they vaped."

I went perfectly still. Pulling a tendril of my keeper magics forward, I sent it his way to cover his tall, slender form in silver mist.

He frowned as if recognizing what I was doing. Though, the only way he'd be able to see my energies was if he...

"I'll save you the trouble of trying to read my aura," Pudsnecker said. "I'm a sorcerer, just as you are. And I'm not here for a book signing, though, if we survive what's coming, I'll be happy to do a signing if that will help your little bookstore sell some books."

The "little bookstore" thing rankled as it always did. "Croakies is doing just fine, Mr. Pudsnecker. I just assumed you'd contacted me to sell *your* books. That was the first thing you spoke about when you called me."

His eyes widened, and he seemed to have an "ah-ha" moment. He nodded, folding his well-manicured hands together behind his back. "Yes. I could see why that would be confusing. I'll admit I was indulging in a bit of subterfuge with you. Very well, let's start over, shall we?" He offered me his hand. "Let me introduce myself to you. I'm Archibald Pudsnecker, chief researcher for the Société of Dire Magic." He must have seen me flinch because he held up his hands, palms out in a defensive gesture. "I don't come to you with the power of the Société behind me, I assure you. I come as a friend. Or..." He grinned and his smile seemed somehow familiar. A vision of laughing blue eyes and a matching smile skated across my memory and was gone in the beat of a heart. I shook it off.

"At least I hope to be friends someday soon," he finished.

I shook my head. "I'm confused. You and I have never met before, right?"

His hesitation was brief enough that I thought I might have imagined it. "That is correct."

"But you come to me, a complete stranger and announce you'd like to be friends?"

He cocked his head back and forth as if he didn't quite agree with my statement. I couldn't imagine what part he might disagree with. "It's not quite that simple, but yes, essentially. I'm actually here because I'm aware of a certain faction within the Société, which means you ill. I'd like to help you with that."

Weariness and frustration shortened my temper. I knew I was being unreasonable, but I couldn't seem to help myself. "I don't need your help with Rogers."

His eyes widened slightly as if he was surprised I knew who he was referring to.

"I've handled him before, and I'll handle him again."

Pudsnecker shook his head. "You don't understand…"

"I understand perfectly well, Arch-i-bald," I said, my tone derisive. "I'm not as stupid or as helpless as you seem to think I am." Only *almost* as stupid and helpless. I did an internal sigh. I really needed to rein myself in. I certainly didn't need any more enemies at the Société. "Look, I'm sorry. I know I'm being a witch with a B, as my friend LA says."

He smiled as I'd hoped he would.

"It's just that things are even crazier here than

usual and I'm..." I hesitated, trying to decide exactly what I was. Overwhelmed? Frustrated? Feeling inadequate?

"Tired," Archibald finished for me.

I realized he was right. "Yes. I'm tired. And right at this moment, I'm hangry too. I don't do hangry well, I'm afraid."

Pudsnecker laughed. "You're just like your..." He stopped, flushing red. "...friend Sebille in that."

That forced a laugh from me. "Hangry hobgoblins! If you're comparing my personality to Sebille's, I'm in deep trouble. Cranky is a day at the beach for her. She usually lives in mean and crotchety land."

He chuckled. "Not at all. You are definitely your own form of hangry."

We shared a smile, and something deep inside me relaxed.

"I'll tell you what," Pudsnecker said. "I'll buy dinner and you and I can talk while we eat. I think you might want to include your friend Sebille in the conversation too. She's going to be needed to fix the problem."

My concentration was sidelined by delighted thoughts of egg rolls and sundry other delicious things. I had to jerk myself back to attention. "Problem?" I asked. "You mean Rogers?" I shook my head. "I really do know how to handle him. I appreciate you trying to help but he's not..."

Archibald held up a hand. "Not that problem. I

have no doubt you can handle that little weasel. But the problem I'm speaking of is big enough to draw the council heads at the Société's interest. And I can assure you, if that happens, they'll align against you and your friends. *All* of them."

I read from his stern expression that he was telling me everyone I cared about would be punished. Sebille, Lea, Grym, maybe even Theo. And if the Société put me out of business, it would also affect Hobs, Wicked, and Slimy. I couldn't let that happen. But I needed more information. "Exactly what problem are you referring to?"

He raised dark brown eyebrows, his expression filled with surprise. "After the Naga incident, you still don't realize you have a problem?"

"The monsters?"

When he nodded, I expelled a breath. "I think I have an idea how to stop that. I just need a few quiet moments to think." The artifact had to be at Croakies. And I was guessing it was a book. I just didn't know how to find it short of touching every single artifact in the place.

Tens of thousands of artifacts.

We didn't have that kind of time.

I kept my comment as neutral as possible so as not to give offense. Pudsnecker was definitely keeping me from my quiet time.

Rather than look insulted, he sighed as if relieved. "Then, you've figured it out?"

"I believe I have, yes."

"Oh, thank the goddess. Do you know how to fix it?"

"Not yet, but I'm confident I'll come up with something once I..."

"Yes, yes, have time all by yourself. Naida, dear, I know you're used to working alone. Or at the very least with a very small group of people you trust. I'm asking to be added to that group. At least for this moment in time. Because I believe I can tell you how to fix this particular problem."

He was right. I was used to working alone. I'd been that way since I reached my teens and realized nobody else was willing to help. That I'd managed to get as far as I had in life was both my biggest success and my most obvious failure. I'd grown far too used to working alone. Even while slowly gathering people around me who *were* willing to help.

"Okay, I'll go get Sebille. I hope you're flush with cash, though, because the sprite and I can put away a lot of egg rolls."

"Egg rolls?" he looked like he'd never heard of the things.

"Oh, you're in for a treat. I'll write out an order for the food. Then we'll need frosted brownies for dessert, at least a dozen."

To his credit, Pudsnecker didn't look appalled by the sheer size of my food requests, so I decided I'd add an order of shrimp to our order for Wicked.

Slimy was on his own. There was no way I was requesting bugs with my Chinese food.

But I did have some crickets in the cupboard. He'd be just as delighted with those as the rest of us would be with our food. "I'll go get Sebille."

Pudsnecker nodded. "Make sure to bring the book."

That stopped me in my tracks. I turned back to him. "Book? What book?"

He stared at me for a beat and then slowly blinked. "Ah. So you haven't actually figured it out."

He didn't sound smug, so I didn't take offense from his observation.

Much.

"I don't know about that, but maybe you and I are on different pages." Speaking of books.

He stared at me for a moment and then nodded. "Very well, let me tell you what page I'm on."

I turned back to him, crossing my arms across my chest. I was well aware that it was a defensive posture, but I was okay with that. There was a soft thump as Mr. Wicked jumped down from the sill and trotted over, his round, orange gaze locked on Pudsnecker with decided coldness. I realized in that moment that my cat hadn't come over to greet the man when he'd come inside either. That was mostly unheard of.

"Ribbit!" sayeth the frog. He'd been abandoned, and I needed to go get him. But first, I wanted to hear what page Pudsnecker was on so I could rip it out of the book. Okay, so I might not be fully in a cooperating mood. "Go ahead," I told him.

The man eyed Wicked thoughtfully and then glanced up at me, his gaze filled with concern. "Your most useful Keeper's tool has been compromised."

I narrowed my gaze. "What's that, now?"

"The Keeper's Book of Possibilities."

When I continued to look confused, he waved a dismissive hand in front of his face. "Sorry. I believe you call it the Book of Pages?"

"Ribbit!"

12

I THOUGHT MY JOB SUCKED LEMONS

*M*y heart thumped once hard against my ribs and then seemed to stop working. My lungs clenched down on whatever air I had left in them. My blood ran cold. And I reached down to scoop up my cat, whose fur had lifted all along his back. "I..."

"I know this is probably a shock..."

"That's impossible," I finally wrenched out through stiff lips.

"I assure you it's not."

"Why? How?" I glanced toward the table and saw the book lying there, though I was certain I'd put it away earlier to keep it safe.

"Your friends recently misused the book to find you in another dimension and bring you back, correct?"

I grimaced. "I wouldn't say they misused it."

"You might not say it, Naida, but it would still be the truth."

I sighed, my fingers digging into Wicked's soft fur, kneading it to calm my nerves. "Okay, they might have used it in ways it wasn't supposed to be used, but..."

"And then a Seer from that dimension meddled further to create a space in time where you could utilize the magics Rustin the ethereal witch created to find and bring you back."

That time I didn't even argue. Gus, the Seer in Plex, had indeed used his antique watch thing to give us more time. "Yes," I said, my voice cracking with emotion.

The monsters were all my fault.

My knees buckled and I dropped into the nearest chair, still clutching Mr. Wicked against my chest. It was a testament to how upset I was that he hadn't smacked me with a partially exposed claw and jumped down yet. "What have we done?"

Archibald sighed. "I don't tell you this to make you feel bad. Sometimes we must use magic in ways it isn't meant to be used. We twist. We shape. We manipulate in the hopes it will give us what we want. There is always a cost to such manipulations. But there are times when the cost is worth it."

I shook my head, unable to verbalize my emotions. Poor Devard. It was all my fault he'd lost the battle with his Naga.

Archibald walked over and gently clasped my shoulder, giving it a squeeze. "We will make this right, Naida dear. You and I and your friends."

I sniffled, realizing too late that tears were sliding down my cheeks. "I'm the world's worst Keeper."

To my surprise, Archibald chuckled. "Not even close, dear. Remind me sometime to tell you about Reggie Wayne. Reggie was far and away the worst Artifact Keeper ever to hold the title."

"Is that supposed to make me feel better?" I sniffled again and scraped tears off my cheeks with the heel of my hand.

Wicked rubbed his head under my chin and started to purr.

"I don't expect it should," Archie admitted. "But it's true. You are not a bad Keeper. In fact, you have the potential to be very good. You just haven't been given all the resources you require to do your job properly. I've put in a request for your trainer to be recalled. She did a terrible job and must be made to remedy her mistakes."

The idea of being a student again after years of bumbling along on my own was both terrifying and comforting. Because I was too emotional to form a definite reaction, I said nothing.

Having a sudden, horrible thought, I looked at Archibald. "Has this fissure been there since we got back from Plex?"

He frowned. "Probably not. Your friends most

likely weakened the Book's void energies performing their magic, but if you haven't noticed the monsters until recently, I'm guessing that was when the breach occurred."

I nodded, feeling marginally better.

"Now, let's get some food ordered and begin planning. The sooner we can remedy this monster situation, the sooner you can get back to your other work."

Again, that didn't make me feel better. I was almost afraid to go into the library and look at the stack of new orders which had come in since I'd left that morning. But I simply nodded, too drained to push back, and carried my cat through the dividing door with me.

Are you forgetting something? a snotty voice asked in my mind. I screeched to a halt, turning back. "Would you do me a favor and put the frog into his terrarium?" I asked my guest.

"Certainly. I've heard a lot about your Mr. Slimy. I look forward to getting to know him better."

Well. That didn't give me pause. No, it did not.

Archibald sat back with a look of wonder on his face as Sebille and I polished off a dozen egg rolls between us. Wicked had long since finished his grilled shrimp and was back on the windowsill, cleaning his paws and keeping one ear cocked toward Devard's place.

Hobs had a chocolate mustache from his dinner of four fat, gooey brownies and was sitting atop the bookshelves feeding bits of bread to his army of songbirds.

We were like a Hallmark flippin' special. Super-normal style.

The sprite had been understandably reticent with my new best pal, but the offer of food had gone a long way to soften her up. And when he started to explain his theory about the Book of Pages, she looked extremely interested. Since I hadn't been there when she and Rustin had "manipulated" the book's magics to find me in Plex, I couldn't add much to their astoundingly complex magical conversation.

My sole contribution was the occasional, "Wow," or "Yikes!" Not very helpful, but they seemed satisfied with my level of discourse. I was mostly just interested in stuffing food into my face as fast as I could.

"So, Archie," the sprite said, her brow knitting, "you think the Book sprung a leak?"

Archibald blinked in surprise at her use of the nickname, but then a smile twitched his lips and he nodded. "In a manner of speaking, yes." He picked up his fork and stabbed it into the mound of fried rice on his plate, seeming as uninterested in eating as Sebille and I were ravenous. "The book retains the collective imaginations, memories, and experiences of the inhabitants of each dimension, holding them in a structured repository of carefully labeled folders whose contents can only be formed into specific items or areas upon request. Normally, the contents of the abyss must be requested by a Keeper. But, there is likely a breach in the magics near the folder for fictional monsters. The breach is allowing monsters to leak out rather than offering them to you as it normally would, by request only. When you manipulated the seeking magics, I believe you inadvertently tore the magic, leaving it open to random suggestion."

I frowned. "Random suggestion?"

He shrugged. "A child down the street watches that children's show with the big blue monster on it, and the big blue monster becomes reality."

Sebille nodded, getting excited. "Someone's afraid of spiders..."

"And a long-forgotten spider monster from goddess knows where appears. Yes." Archibald agreed.

"I'm guessing Theo's been admiring his *Dance of the Monsters* clock recently," I said, finally understanding. "So, how do we fix a tear in the book? Slap some tape over it?"

Archie laughed. "I truly wish it were that easy, child." He pushed his rice away. "No, the fix will be more involved than that. And more dangerous." He lifted a tidy brown brow. "Are you up for it?"

I shrugged. "It's my job."

My response seemed to please him. "Yes. Of course." He looked at Sebille. She appeared offended. "It's my job too."

"Excellent! We'll need your ethereal friend too," he told me.

"Rustin?"

"Yes. And that roughhewn police detective as well. It will be all hands on deck for this one."

The way he grinned, I wondered if he wasn't enjoying the idea of my friends and I plunging into danger just a bit too much.

I had a sudden thought and frowned at the sorcerer. "You're the one who closed the order on the monster artifact, weren't you?"

Archie sighed. "I had to do it. If it became known at the Société that your Book of Possibilities is the culprit, you'd be seen as having lost control of one of your most important Keeper tools."

And I'd be toast.

I didn't like it, but I understood. "Tell us what we need to do to fix this," I urged again.

"Yes, the details. Of course." He gave it a moment's thought and then leaned forward, placing his forearms on the table. "The trick is finding the breach. There's only one way it can be done. When it's open and active."

"What does that mean, exactly?" I asked, feeling stupid.

But Sebille had been following more closely than I had. She caught his meaning right away. "While there's a monster present."

"Precisely," Archibald said, clapping his hands.

The birds lifted off the shelves in alarm, fluttering around over our heads for a beat before settling back around Hobs, who still had bread in his hand.

"While the monster is active, we'll need the detective and your Rustin to contain it while you two enter the book to plug the breach."

"How will we find the breach?" Thinking of the angry witch we'd trapped there, I didn't relish the idea of wandering around the abyss looking for a small hole in the magic.

"While the monster is active, the Book should open to the exact spot he came from. Or it should, at the very least, be near the breach."

"And if it doesn't?" Sebille asked.

"That would be unfortunate indeed. Let's focus on the better outcome for now. We'll have to adjust on the fly if it doesn't work."

I had a terrible thought. My gaze skimming to Sebille, I put words to my horror. "Jacob Quilleran!"

She paled, her abundance of freckles like glowing dots on her colorless face. She skimmed a look toward our guest. "We trapped a powerful witch in the abyss. Is it possible he could get out through this breach?"

Archibald pursed his lips, looking uncomfortable. He didn't even need to respond. I read his concern in the way he shifted in his chair. "We'll want to work as quickly as possible to avoid that outcome."

Putrid Pixie pustules! "We can't let him escape," I told Archibald. "He could cause so much more trouble than any of these monsters ever could."

Sebille nodded her agreement. "If the breach has been in place for a couple of days now, isn't it possible he's already gotten out?"

Our new friend stared at his rejected rice for too long before giving us a sigh. "I'm not going to lie to you. I know about Jacob Quilleran. He's smart and he's not the type to just sit in the abyss and feel sorry for himself. I can all but guarantee that he's been actively searching for a way out since the moment you trapped him there."

Sebille and I shared a look. My heart slammed against my chest in instant panic. Silvery stars beat against the front of my eyeballs with violent enthusiasm. The sprite didn't look much better.

"But, having said that, the abyss is an endless space without time. It's why we call it the abyss. The chances of him finding this one, small breach in the amount of time he's had available to him are slim. Extremely slim. So why don't we just focus on closing the breach as quickly as possible? Hopefully, that will take care of the Quilleran problem."

His response was calm and it was logical. I knew he was right. I also knew there was nothing we could do to fix it if Jacob Quilleran had already escaped.

But none of that made me feel any better.

"How do we get a monster to come through when we want it to?" Sebille asked him.

Archibald placed a hand on the Book of Pages, which was sitting in the center of the table, where it had been safe from flying food while Sebille and I had chawed through the existing egg rolls like termites through decaying wood. "That, my dears, is the easy part. All we need to do, I believe, is to try to use the book as usual, thinking of a monster."

"Preferably one that's not too scary," I offered.

Archibald looked at me, but he didn't laugh.

Dithering dingo dung! "You have more bad news for me, don't you?"

He sighed. "I am sorry. But you have no control over the monster that comes through. The very nature of this flaw in the system is that it is random. And, with every creature that comes through, the creatures it sends next will be worse and harder to vanquish."

His words were terrifying, but they brought a question to my mind. "Wait a minute. The last monster we dealt with was the Naga. It didn't come from the abyss. The Naga is part of our friend Devard. It's his magical side."

Archibald shook his head. "Devard Othco was cursed by a wizard many decades ago. His Naga is not part of him. It's not his magic to call. His curse lives in the abyss, and only his extreme control over the triggers that bring it forth keep the monster away most of the time. That, and his one concession to its existence."

"Concession?" Sebille asked.

Archibald sighed. "One month out of every year, Devard allows the monster to reign supreme. And, in order for the world to be safe from the creature because he has no control over it once it rises to the surface, he goes into the abyss for that month."

I frowned, thinking about Sebille once telling me that Devard took a yearly vacation for a month, spending it at some undisclosed location. Sebille speculated that he went to some beach somewhere, soaking up the sun and drinking fruity drinks.

Knowing the truth of that month made me want to give Devard a hug.

I saw a similar sentiment blossom on Sebille's long, freckled face.

"How sad," I said.

Archibald nodded.

"But then, how does he get back from the abyss?" Sebille asked. "And how do you know all this?" Her second question was filled with suspicion. She looked upon Archibald Pudsnecker with a narrowed gaze.

Archie shook his head. "Unfortunately, the answer to both questions is, me," he told us. "I'm a sorcerer, and my magic to call is geared toward management of voids."

"Wait," I said. "Your job is to monitor vacant areas in the Universe?"

He nodded.

I reached over and patted him on the shoulder. "And I thought my job sucked lemons."

13

HASTA LA VISTA, BABY

*A*fter further discussion, we decided to attempt the breach repair first thing in the morning. When Archie had left, I called Grym and Rustin. They agreed to come to Croakies at dawn to do their part against whatever nightmare emerged from the abyss.

Then Sebille and I stood in the bookstore, looking at each other.

It was the moment of truth. I had to go up to my apartment, and I feared what I'd find there. The last time Sebille had stayed with me, I'd needed a GPS tracker to find my way through all her furniture to my bed. Forget making it to the bathroom to sing the *Make me a Magic Muffin Mister* song.

I was tired and wired at the same time. Making a sudden decision, I said, "I think I'm too keyed up to sleep. I'm going to see if there's an artifact order I can tackle."

Sebille nodded. "I was thinking the same thing. Let's go see what we can find."

As she reached for the dividing door, I realized I hadn't heard the clanging in a while. My heart soared. Maybe the orders had finally stopped! I shared my hopes with Sebille.

As usual, she slammed a virtual fist into them.

"I inserted a noise dampening spell between the library and the store." She tugged the door open, and the first thing I heard was a muffled, *Clangggggggggggg.*

I sighed. "I haven't even looked at the orders since this morning. How bad is it?"

"Not too bad, actually. I put Hobs to work gathering up the orders as they arrived." She reached out and caught the new one that was fluttering toward the ground and glanced at it, frowning. "Oh no,"

My pulse picked up. We didn't need any "oh no's" at the moment. "What now?"

She turned a stricken look on me. "I can't believe it."

Sweat slicked my palms. I suddenly found it hard to breathe. "Tell me before I pass out."

She held the sheet up and shook it. "I love this place."

I took the order and quickly scanned it, finding

the name of the artifact to be collected at the bottom. Recognition flared. "I knew it!"

Sebille scowled over at me. "You don't have to look so happy about it," she groused. "Can't we just pretend we never saw that?"

My grin made her groan. "I might not be much as an artifact keeper, Sebille. But I have my standards and my word. I pledged to find and wrangle all artifacts it was within my ability to wrangle, and I meant it."

"Blah, blah, blah," Sebille groused, looking cranky. "*You* can handle that one. I think it would break my heart."

I nodded. "Let's grab one more. If we have time, we'll tackle two of them tonight."

She grabbed the one off the top of the pile, which I noted had grown to be almost as high as my arm was long.

Weariness swept through me at the sight.

"I told Hobs to stack them oldest to newest. Oldest on the top."

I nodded. Good idea. "Which one is that?"

"That stupid Groundhog's Day clock. It's been here almost four days."

I winced. "Okay, let's tackle that first then."

She brightened. "Good. Maybe we'll run out of time to do the other one."

The man who'd been the unfortunate recipient of the Groundhog's Day alarm clock lived on the third floor of a nondescript apartment building on the South side of Enchanted. It was a fairly rough area with a questionable element in the form of street gangs. The police had fought a losing battle over the gangs for years because they didn't understand what they were dealing with. If Grym's boss had allowed him and his hand-picked supernormal cops to handle the gang problem, it would be quickly solved. But Chief Pinteck didn't know about supernormals. In his mind, the gang was comprised of a bunch of thugs and reprobates. The supernormal world recognized the group of wizards for what they were. Deadly and unscrupulous. And brimming with power they hadn't grown into yet. Wizards generally didn't reach what the supernormal world considered adulthood until they'd lived for sixty years. Most of the young gang members were in their forties. A few in their fifties. To humans, they looked like they were twenty. Thus, a police force that didn't know magic existed thought what they had was a dangerous and annoying group of young thugs on their hands. What they really had was a disaster waiting to happen.

The wizards, which in a metaphorical middle finger to the cops was the name of the gang too, trafficked in stolen magic and artifacts. They generally sold their goods in the bigger cities around Enchanted, where most police forces had special groups like Grym's to handle the woo-woo stuff. Even if they didn't recognize it as magic, the larger force of cops meant more supernormals in the ranks. More supernormal cops meant more trouble for a gang that only thrived because the cops didn't recognize how truly dangerous they were. The wizards did business in those cities, but they chose to live where the police didn't recognize what they were. It was safer for them in Enchanted.

They might be young but they weren't stupid.

Well, not about that anyway.

We pulled up in front of the apartment and I parked my little bug at the curb. It had started to rain since we'd left Croakies, and a mist was rising from the ground as temps changed. Two men stood on the stoop leading to the apartments. They were smoking something that probably wasn't tobacco and the men were way too interested in us as we climbed out.

Wizards.

Frog flippin' wonderful.

I looked at the hobgoblin, cat, and frog in the back seat. "Maybe you guys should stay here."

Eyeing the two men, who'd taken a step down from the stoop and were standing shoulder to shoulder in front of the door, blocking it, Sebille said. "Maybe we should all stay here."

Ignoring me as only a cat can do, Wicked jumped out of the car and trotted up the sidewalk with his tail held high. Hobs shot past Sebille, leaving a blur on the air and a squishy frog in the sprite's hands. She looked down with a frown. "I hate when he does that."

I shrugged my brows. "It does come in useful, though."

One of the wizards elbowed the other one, a mean smile splitting his face. "Hey, look, George, it's a kitty cat."

The other wizard took a long drag on his "cigarette", his gaze locked on mine and something ugly in the twist of his lips. "I like me some kitty cat," George said in a suggestive tone.

Ice formed along my spine. I looked at Sebille. "Maybe this wasn't such a good idea."

To my surprise, she was grinning back. "I wouldn't underestimate that kitty, if I were you," Sebille told the magical thugs.

The first wizard widened his gaze as he looked the sprite over. She was dressed in her usual fashion. Her long bright blue dress hit her about mid-shin, covering the tops of a pair of socks that reached to her bony knees in wide stripes. The current socks were fairly mundane in black and white, but the puffy coat she wore over the blue dress was mustard yellow. An unfortunate color when worn with her shiny red Wicked Witch of the West shoes. But the shoes went well with her fire-red hair, which she'd pulled into a single thick braid that trailed down to the small of her back.

"George, I think somebody exploded a paint company, and it turned into a girl."

George finally scraped his gaze from me and eyed Sebille. He blinked slowly, like a lizard, and then looked at his hand-wrapped cigarette. "Maybe we should lay off this stuff for a while," he told his friend. "The world's gone psychedelic."

The friend burst out laughing.

The air around them blurred in shades of white, green, and red. When it cleared, the friend was gone.

George blinked again and then frowned.

"George!" a muffled voice called out.

We all lifted our gazes to find George's friend hanging upside down from a leafless tree down the street.

Standing on the branch above him, Hobs waved at us with the hand that wasn't holding the thug.

Rage transforming his face at the sight of his friend's predicament, George threw down his smokable and turned to us.

Watch out, said the frog. *He's reaching for energy.*

Sebille's hand snapped out, and she threw a thick bolt of green magic in the wizard's direction. But George was too fast for her. His hand flew up and oily black mist oozed from his palm. Sebille's energy hit the black ooze and was swallowed.

She handed Slimy to me and threw another bolt, but the results were the same.

We were in trouble. My magics weren't defensive. Though I had things I could call that were.

Wicked stopped a few feet away from George and sat, the orange light from his soul star sigil, which I couldn't see burning from where I stood, bathed the wet concrete in front of him. I felt a tug in the core of my magic and it shot toward my fingertips, silvery energy escaping to snap against the moist air.

George's lips opened in a wide smile, showing small, stained teeth with a large gap between the larger ones in the center. "You ladies don't have what it takes to beat me. All you're going to do is make me mad."

"Slavering centipedes," I murmured. With a sigh, I flung out my hand and sent my keeper magics into the mist. It shot away on a whistle of air and disappeared between the buildings on the street.

Too late, I realized my mistake. The night erupted in a series of answering chimes, warning me that I'd probably bitten off more than I could chew.

The first artifact slammed into my car and clattered to the ground.

Three more appeared from the mist and Sebille

and I ducked just in time to avoid being hit by those too.

I heard the next one coming from a distance, the whistling sound of my magic carrying it our way was louder than usual, which told me the object was heavier than the others.

Awesome sauce.

I lifted my hand and a dark, metallic object slammed into my palm. It hurt. Bees bunions did it hurt...but I was pleased with myself that I hadn't let it clock me in the head.

I wasn't pleased for long when I saw what it was, though.

Magic hissed on the air and three long daggers appeared from the mist and stabbed into the ground around Wicked.

He didn't so much as flinch.

I watched in surprise as, one by one, the blades lifted from the grass and shot toward the wizard.

That was new. *Go Wicked.*

The wizard threw his oily magic at the knives and they stopped, wriggling in the air between George and Mr. Wicked as the two magics battled for control.

Sebille flung another bolt of energy at the thug, but he threw up his left hand and devoured her magic with another cloud of oily energy.

She threw another bolt, and another, and another, moving steadily toward him as she fired.

He swung his arm and Wicked and his magicked knives flew sideways. I winced in sympathy as my cat hit a nearby bush with a yowl of pain.

George started forward, his magic bolts matching Sebille's strike for strike. Finally, when they were only a few feet apart, he threw up both hands and sent a dense wall of the oily black energy at the sprite. The nasty power picked Sebille up and threw her toward the same bush from which Wicked was currently trying to extricate himself.

Then all that was standing between the wizard and me was a frog and a gun artifact.

Shoot him, sayeth the frog.

All the blood left my face. "I can't just shoot him."

George laughed, a new batch of ugly energy gathering in his hands.

I felt Slimy roll his eyes in my mind. Or maybe I was just channeling Sebille for a beat. I don't know. But I could tell he was disgusted.

It's him or us, Naida.

Then it might have to be us, I thought back at him. *I don't know if I can shoot him with this gun.*

There are no bullets, the frog told me, his voice filled with disgust. *It's magic. It won't kill him.*

You don't know that.

Yes, I do, he countered.

During our mental argument, the wizard had moved a lot closer. Dense black energy boiled in his palms. I suspected if he hit me with that magic, it was going to really hurt, or worse. I had to do something.

Shoot him! the frog insisted.

George's eyes gleamed with malice. His lips curved. He lifted his hands and said, "*Hasta la vista*, baby." And he flung his hands forward.

I screamed, pointed the gun at him, and pulled the trigger.

George's eyes went wide. He flew into the air. His body twisted, spun, and became wrapped in its own magic. Then, accompanied by George's terrified bellow, the twisted length of his body shot in my direction, heading right for the gun in my hand, and was sucked into the barrel of the weapon.

The force of him hitting the gun was like being punched with a gargoyle fist. I slammed into the side of my car with a resounding "bang!"

Pain radiated across my back, digging its claws deep into my bones, and I struggled to pull air into my lungs.

It took me a moment to realize what had happened.

I told you to shoot him, sayeth the frog.

I sat forward, trying to decide if anything was broken, and groaned as pain radiated down my back. Realizing I was still holding the gun, I dropped it. "Yeah," I told Slimy. "Great idea."

He harrumphed, apparently not liking the tone

of my voice. *Now, do you think you can pull me out of the gutter?*

I looked around, finding his shiny black gaze peering at me from beneath the curb. I must have dropped him when the wizard's body hit the muzzle of the gun. "Yikes. Sorry about that."

A piece of prickly green leaf fluttered to the ground in front of me. I looked up at Sebille. She was covered in scratches and pieces of prickly bush stuck out of her hair in a type of crown. I couldn't help it, I grinned. "I like the crown. You look like your mother."

Sindra, Queen of the Enchanted Fae.

"Har, de, har, har, Naida," she said grumpily. "Can we get this stupid clock and get out of here?"

I nodded and pushed to my feet. Extracting the frog from the gutter, I looked around for my cat.

"Wicked's already in the car. Hobs too," Sebille informed me. "They scampered over and climbed in after you sucked that guy into the gun." She gave me a reluctant grin. "That was icy."

Despite myself, I smiled back. "Yeah, it was." I frowned at the weapon in the frosty grass. "Now, I just need to figure out how to extract him."

"Later would be better for that," the sprite said. "Much later. Maybe Archie will have an idea how to do it."

That made sense. Chances were good that the wizard was in some kind of void. "Okay." I opened the car door and placed Slimy on the dashboard. "Hobs, can you pick all these artifacts up and put them on the floor of the car?"

"Yes, Miss," agreed Hobs. The hobgoblin scrambled back out of the car and started picking up artifacts.

"If we're lucky," I told Sebille, "we'll have orders for these back at Croakies." It might save hours of work later.

"Hey!" said an angry voice behind me.

I whipped around to find George's friend, looking a little wobbly on his feet. Shaky and pale he might be, but that didn't stop him from gathering a bunch of oily energy in his palms. "Tell me what you did with George. Now!"

"Hobs?" Sebille extended her hand toward the hobgoblin and Hobs gave her the gun. "I'll do you one better." She said. "I'll show you." She pulled the trigger and the guy flew off the ground on a startled cry. He twisted, spun, and shot toward the gun, slamming into the barrel.

Sebille must have witnessed the weapon's kickback when I'd used it, because she'd braced for impact and, as a result, was only forced backward a couple of steps.

With a wide grin, she blew on the end of the gun. "I'm likin' this one, Naida."

I couldn't disagree. It had recently become my favorite artifact too.

W e stood in front of a battered wooden door with the number 666 written in thick black ink at eye level. I shook my head. "Funny."

Sebille chuckled.

Since we were on the third floor and none of the other doors had six hundred numbers, the occult-ish number was a sick joke.

Sebille lifted her fist to knock as it flew open. "Thank the goddess!" The scrawny, red-eyed man with suitcases under his eyes shoved the alarm clock into my arms. I've tried to go murder that stupid groundhog a dozen times over the last week, but those jerks always had the front door blocked and wouldn't let me out. I'm assuming you'll take care of this?"

By "this" I figured he meant the alarm clock. "I'll take care of the clock, but the Keeper's office doesn't sanction murdering groundhogs."

He glowered at me, his gaze level with mine despite the fact that I was only five foot six inches tall. "That's because you haven't had your life turned inside out and upside down for six days by that stupid rodent."

I could feel Sebille holding in a laugh.

I bit my bottom lip to keep from smiling too. "Go

get some sleep. When you wake up in the morning, there will be no Groundhog Day."

"Thank the goddess," he muttered ungratefully, before slamming the door in our faces.

We headed for the stairs with our treasure. "One down, one thousand and counting to go," I said with a fake smile.

Sebille grunted. "Please tell me we're not going to try to tackle the next one?"

I knew what she was up to. She just didn't want to take out her favorite snack spot. "Not tonight. I guess the population of Enchanted will just continue to be manipulated by that particular magic for another day."

Sebille did a fist pump. "I'm wondering if Lea would make me a memory spell to help you forget about that order."

I laughed, knowing my friend the witch would definitely give that some thought. It was her favorite snack spot too. "Don't even go there, sprite."

At the stairs leading to my apartment, Sebille kept walking as I started climbing. I turned in surprise. "Aren't you going to bed? We need to get up in about four hours."

She yawned, nodding. "Yep. I'll see you in the morning."

Feeling only a tiny bit guilty for doing a little happy dance, I started up the stairs. Sebille had apparently found another place to put down roots—and couches, and tables, and curio shelves, and too many chairs for one person to *ever* use. I danced up the stairs. The sprite would be wearing her red and white striped onesies in another spot in the building. Far away from me and my beloved stuff. She'd be doing her little whistle-snore in a place far, far away from my soon-to-be-blissfully-sleeping form.

Joy became a living thing in my chest. Birds sang from vibrant green trees in my mind. Water trickled happily...

Footsteps pounded up behind me, followed by cackling laughter. "Gotcha! First one upstairs gets the bathroom."

My spirits crashed around my feet as I watched the sprite beating me through the door to my once tranquil abode. I trudged after her, feeling as if someone had pooped dragon-sized dung onto my parade.

14

IT'S A BEAUTIFUL DAY IN THE FROG FLIPPIN' NEIGHBORHOOD

I sat bleary-eyed at the table in the bookstore. My eyes were weighted by lack of sleep, my thoughts muzzy. It was all I could do to lift the teacup to my mouth to sip.

I was pretty sure I was asleep and didn't know it.

"Good morning!" the sprite chirped happily.

My response was a glower, followed by a glare, frosted with a scowl. She was *never* happy. Especially not in the morning. And most especially after only four hours of sleep.

She was tweakin' me. Wringing my last nerve.

Why I oughta...

The door jangled happily as Rustin walked in. Goddess bless his bright soul, he was carrying a greasy box filled with something that smelled like an extra inch or two on my hips.

I held out a hand, grunting like a zombie. "Gimme!"

He laughed, dropping the box on the table in front of me.

Like a plague of locusts, the living and breathing inhabitants of Croakies descended on the box. There was a whir of movement, some shuffling and growling, and then the locusts went their separate ways.

I looked into the empty box, wondering if I could wring some energy from the grease spot.

Rustin silently held out a bag. "I got your back," he said, smiling.

"Marry me," I responded. I grudgingly offered him a donut from the bag and then perused my choices before picking the biggest, most chocolatey pastry. I bit into it and moaned with pleasure. The burst of sugar and fat gave my weary system an immediate jolt.

The door jangled again, saving Rustin from having to respond to my ill-advised proposal. After all, he was a man without a body and I was a sorceress without sleep who would probably die over the next few hours. What kind of future would we have?

Did it even matter if there were donuts available?

Hmmm, deep thoughts. Too deep for so early in the morning.

Walking into Croakies, Grym nodded at Rustin, eyeing the bag I was jealously guarding. After a moment he sighed. "I guess you don't need these?" He pulled another greasy box out from where he'd been hiding it behind his back.

The locusts swarmed again.

Grym stumbled back under the attack, yanking his hand away at the last moment to check if all his fingers were still intact.

When it cleared, my cat bounced away with a glazed donut between his teeth. Hobs spun back toward the library with his arms full of chocolate donuts, and Sebille clutched the biggest pastry I'd ever seen in one hand.

With a grin, she offered it to Grym. "It was the only way to save you one."

He took it gratefully. "I guess I'll learn someday not to bring a box of donuts into this place without packing some serious protection."

Sebille chuckled, glancing at Rustin. "Where's Sadie?"

"I left her at home until I hear what we're doing. I thought she'd be safer there."

The sprite nodded in agreement. "I'll make tea."

Once Sebille was seated and we all had tea, Grym asked the obvious question. "So, what do you need from us today?"

I wished I knew. "I'm afraid you're going to be fighting another monster."

"What kind of monster?" Rustin asked. "I'll need to prepare."

Grimacing, I looked at Sebille.

"According to Archie, we won't know what the abyss is going to send us until it's here. But he said the monsters will keep getting worse each time one arrives."

"So we need to make sure we get this shut down," I told them, frowning. "I can't imagine anything worse than the Naga."

A grim silence fell over the room.

As if on cue, the door opened again and Archie Pudsnecker stood there, looking every bit a Sorcerer of the Voids. He was dressed in a thick, black cloak with oversized sleeves that hung past his elegant hands. His dark blue gaze shone with emotion and his stride when he entered the room, was brisk. "Are we ready to get started?"

"No," we all said at once.

He blinked, looked from one to the other of us, and then frowned. "What's the problem?"

Grym laughed. "What's the problem? Where do I start. To begin, if we don't know what kind of monster we're going to be dealing with, how can we prepare?"

Rustin nodded. "What kind of protection will Naida and Sebille have inside the book? They don't know where they're going, or how they're going to fix the breach and there's a dangerous witch in the abyss. How are they going to protect themselves against Jacob Quilleran?"

The way Rustin spoke of his uncle, I realized he'd cut any emotional ties he'd had with the man. Probably a good idea. "Can Sebille and I take any kind of weapons with us?" I asked, thinking of the gun we'd gotten from the wizards. That particular artifact would definitely come in handy in the abyss.

Then I blinked, thinking of the two men we'd sucked up with the gun. Would they be waiting for us when we entered the abyss too? "Um, how big is the abyss?"

Everyone looked at me, varying degrees of "you're kidding, right?" written across their faces.

I shrugged. "It's not as stupid a question as it sounds..." I started to say.

"Yes, it is," Sebille told me. "The abyss is endless."

Archie shook his head. "It's both endless and extremely contracted."

"Explain," Rustin said, as if asking a professor to give more detail on a homework assignment.

Sighing, Archie held up his hands. "The best way I can explain it to you is this. Think of it as neighborhoods. Each of us has ties to a section of the abyss. Our neighborhood, so to speak. And when we interact, we tend to interact with our own neighborhood. But when dealing with the Book, that effect is muted somewhat. The Book touches all segments of the abyss. Its power spreads across the entire thing."

Okay, then hopefully Jacob wouldn't be an issue.

But the wizards... I saw no way around it. I had to fess up to what Sebille and I had done. "We went looking for an artifact last night," I told the three men. I received a variety of reactions to my statement, from impatience in the sorcerer, to immediate suspicion from the gargoyle, to concern from the ghost witch.

I hurried on. "It was on the south end of Enchanted."

That shoved suspicion off Grym's face and replaced it with concern. The sorcerer still looked impatient.

"When we got to the location where the artifact was located, there were two wizards blocking the door."

Grym shook his head. "I keep telling the Chief that we need to do something about those gangs."

I nodded. "I tried to avoid confrontation by using my power to call the artifacts in the area." I grimaced. "We got back a lot of weapons. Several knives, some brass knuckles, a stun gun and some mace..." I slid my gaze to Archie. "And a gun that sucks the bad guys into the abyss."

Archie's face paled. "Let me see if I have this right. You sucked two combative wizards into the abyss last night?"

I nodded. "My question is this. Will we bump into them when we go in to fix the breach?"

Archie sighed. "Most certainly. Unlike the Book,

any artifact you use to put someone into the void would send them into your neighborhood there."

"But we don't know the Book will send Naida close to her neighborhood," Rustin argued.

"No. We don't. But the global touch of the artifact only applies to specific requests. If you specifically request a certain place or person, the book will take you there regardless of where in the void it is. But if you don't specify…"

"It will pick your neighborhood," Rustin said, looking a bit gray around the gills. "I need to go in with them," he finally said.

Archie shook his head. "I don't advise it, son. I know you're worried about the two young women, but I assure you, if I didn't think they could handle this, I wouldn't send them inside."

I chewed on my lip, wishing I had half the confidence in me that the sorcerer had.

"We'll take Wicked," Sebille said. "And Hobs."

The exterior door blew open and a tiny rainbow shot through, wings beating the air rapidly as she hovered before Rustin, chittering emphatically.

I couldn't understand a word the little dragon was saying, but the gist of her message was clear. She was mad at Rustin for leaving her behind.

Rustin chittered back in an attempt to plead his case, but the little dragon would have none of it. She blew smoke in his face and flew over to land on Sebille's shoulder.

Rustin sighed. "I guess you're taking Sadie too."

Sebille was torn between happiness and worry.

I settled my gaze on her. "Remember what Kanish told us. Sadie's not a baby. And she apparently has prodigious magical power."

Sebille touched the little dragon's snout with her nose. "Okay. We'll take her. If nothing else, she'll be a nice surprise for those wizard jerks if they try anything."

"Good," Archie said. "Then, we're ready to get started."

Grym held up a hand. "I need to get my people here."

"No humans," Archie said, shaking his head.

"They're not human," Grym told him. "And it's not up for debate."

Sighing, Archie flipped a hand toward the gargoyle, dismissing him. Grym left the store, already speaking on his phone as he closed the door behind him.

Then Archie focused his full attention on Sebille and me. Rubbing his hands together, he said. "Let's find that breach, shall we?"

T he book sat on the table in front of me. My palms were sweating as Archie cast it in silvery mist, his eyes closed and his palms open above it as if reading the contents of the thing without even cracking the cover.

I didn't know what he was doing, but I gathered it had something to do with trying to pinpoint the approximate location of the tear in the Book's magic so Sebille and I wouldn't have to search the entire abyss looking for it.

Sebille and I were stuffing supplies into two canvas backpacks. Bottles of water, protein bars and stuff for our critters and Hobs. We'd even stuffed a couple of blankets into each pack, just in case we ended up having to sleep in the abyss.

Goddess forbid.

The thought made me shudder so hard that my teeth clanked together.

Archie's eyes snapped open and I was afraid he'd heard my teeth clanking, but he stepped back from the book and rubbed a weary hand over his eyes. "That should do it. According to my assessment, you'll enter the abyss no farther away than a mile or two from the tear."

That didn't sound very close to me. But I guessed if the void was endless, two miles was a very small area. "How will we know which direction to go?"

Archie poked his own chest. "It will be here. This

is your magic to call, Sorceress. Embrace it, infuse it into your cells. It's every bit as much a part of your strength as your domination of the artifact library is."

I nodded, not really understanding but trusting that the sorcerer knew what he was talking about.

"Before we start," Archie told me, a new tightness in his gaze. "Please be aware that we will widen the breach just by sending you inside the book. While you are inside, it will be wide open for anything nearby to pass through."

I felt my eyes go wide. "You mean more than one monster might come through the opening?"

He inclined his head. "I will do what I can to limit access. Hopefully, that will be enough. But the longer it takes you to find the tear and repair it, the harder it will be for me to hold."

Galloping gargoyles! "No pressure there," I murmured unhappily.

Grym came through the door a moment later, looking like his name. "My people are ranged along the front of the store. They'll help us contain whatever comes through."

My heart beating hard against my ribs, I nodded. My friends would be in danger while I was in the Book. And the longer I took, the more danger they'd be in.

I was standing so deep in dragon dung I'd be plucking it out of my ears for days.

"Ready?" Archie asked.

I barely bit back a denial, nodding even as my stomach twisted with dread.

He jerked his chin toward the book.

I stepped forward and stopped, looking at the sprite, the dragon, Hobs, and Mr. Wicked. The cat was on the table, along with the frog. I hadn't seen him arrive there. "Mr. Slimy can't come."

"Yeow!" Wicked slashed a half-extended claw over my hand.

"Ow!" I frowned at him. "He won't be safe there."

Slimy hopped toward me. *You'll need me there, Naida.*

I stared down at him. He looked so squishy and helpless sitting on the table blinking up at me. The perfect victim. But Wicked knew more about how magic worked than I did. He was better at it than I was too.

Still. "I don't want you to get hurt," I told the frog. Or worse.

You need me, he insisted.

"Why?"

His squish rippled in a froggy shrug. *I don't know. I just know you do.*

"Day is burning, Naida keeper," Archie nudged.

I sighed and scooped up the frog. "All right, frog. But if you get yourself hurt, I'm not going to be happy."

Like it will put a crimp in my day to have you ticked

at me. It would just be business as usual, sayeth the frog.

"Nobody likes a snarky frog," I told him.

We shrugged on our backpacks and gathered near the table. Sebille moved close, grabbing Hobs' hand. Wicked pressed up against my belly. Sadie chittered happily in Sebille's ear. The little dragon was happy no matter where she went. I envied her that. But it was a little harder to be mindlessly happy when the fate of all your friends rested on your narrow, drooping shoulders.

I took a deep breath and reached out to touch the book. At the last moment, Archie touched my hand and said a couple of words.

The magic shot out of the Book of Pages and wrapped around us like a blanket, twisting us in a painful coil, and jerking us away from everything comfortable and safe.

15

A LITTLE ABYSS…A LITTLE OF THAT

*D*uring our journey through the Book, we bumped up against something big and stinky. The unhappy critter roared into my face, painting me with hot, fetid breath that smelled like butt. I got the sensation of giant, snapping teeth before it disappeared.

I hit the ground and rolled to a stop, the ground beneath me much softer than I'd expected, though something was digging painfully into my back. After a moment's contemplation, I realized it was my backpack. I sat up and looked around, aware of Sebille's groans nearby, and the plaintive yowling of my cat.

I found Hobs a few feet away. He leaped to his feet as if someone had set him on fire, and Mr. Wicked crawled to his feet in the spot where Hobs had been. The hobgoblin had landed on my cat.

Ouch! "Is everybody okay?"

Sadie flitted over to me, her wings beating the air behind her as she went vertical, telling me a rapid-fire story in her native dragonish that went right over my head and got lost in the void.

Sebille pushed to her feet, moving slower than usual. "She's fine."

I looked at my assistant, assessing her for obvious wounds. She brushed grass off her purple dress and looked down at her green and white striped socks, grimacing at the grass stains polluting her knees. "You understood her?"

Sebille looked up, frowned slightly, and then smiled. "I did."

I nodded. "It was like that for me with Slimy on Plex." *Slimy*! I shoved a hand into my pocket, afraid of what I'd find there.

It was empty!

"Slimy? Where are you?"

"Ribbit!" I found him a few feet away, crouched next to a tall bunch of weeds, tongue happily snapping up crickets.

I shook my head. "You always land on your feet, frog."

"Ribbit."

'Nuff said.

Wicked trotted over and rubbed his silky head against my calf. His purring was loud enough to draw unwanted attention, even in the void. I kissed my cat between his twitching gray ears and scooped up the frog, glancing around. The area was very similar to Enchanted Park, with lush tree cover and wide expanses of thick, green grass. In the distance, I even saw the familiar shape of the pavilion where we'd defeated a scary goddess and fought bunnies and squirrels to get Maleficent's staff back.

Yeah, my life is pure chaos. All. The. Dang. Time.

The spot where we'd landed clearly represented the park. It wasn't the same, though, because everything was muted behind a constantly moving wall of gray mist.

When I'd gone into the Book to speak to Rustin beneath the clock tower the first time, I'd assumed the mist was part of the place where I'd landed. With the enormous tower hanging over our heads and the roiling mist, the place had a historical London vibe, and I couldn't help thinking of Jack the Ripper's misty nighttime terrors in England's most well-known city.

But I was starting to realize the mist might be more a part of the abyss and less a component of any individual place there.

I filed that useless bit of information away in my brain and looked around, wondering if the "neighborhood" we'd be exploring in the void would be laid out like the area in Enchanted it represented.

"So. Where to, oh great breach tracker," Sebille asked.

I glanced her way and raised my brows. Sadie

was sitting on top of the sprite's head, her bright gaze glowing eerily through the mist.

Sebille shrugged. "She says she can see better up there."

I bit back a laugh. "Right. Okay, so..." I spun around again. Looking. Looking. Spun again. Looked some more. Spun. Looked...

"You're making me dizzy, Naida!" Sebille barked.

I jumped and grabbed my chest. "Don't yell. We don't want to attract those wizards if we can help it."

"Then we should get moving, shouldn't we?"

I rubbed my chest, indigestion making it hurt. The sprite's cranky brand of brutal common sense was not sitting well at all. "I'm trying, Sebille."

"Meow!" my cat said. I turned to find him jumping on an oversized grasshopper and chowing down.

I grimaced. "Okay." I waited a beat, sensing nothing.

"Okay?" Sebille said, arching a bright red brow.

"Maybe if I close my eyes..."

Nothing.

"Miss?"

I turned around to find Hobs standing a few feet away, near the trees. "I think I hear something coming."

Panic set in. The acidic bubble in my chest flared hotter, and I belched. "Yikes! Excuse me."

"Nice, Naida," Sebille said, her lip curling.

"Hey," I told her, poking a finger toward my assistant's face. "Unless you want me to record all the sounds and emissions happening when you sleep, you'll shut your trap right now. And, trust me, it's quite the symphony."

Sebille turned gray and lifted her hands in surrender. "Trap shut. Geez, cranky much?"

I gave her an eye roll, feeling empowered from the action.

Sadie shot up from Sebille's head, chittering fast and furious. She flew over to Hobs and back to Sebille and then surged over to me and hung in the air, giving me a frantic warning in sounds I had no hope of ever understanding.

I looked at Sebille. "What's she saying?"

Sebille grabbed my arm. "Come on, something big and nasty is coming our way. We need to hide."

"Where?"

"I don't know, but we need to get out of here for starters."

I nodded. "Come on, Wicked." Silly me. He wasn't where I'd last seen him. He was already running into the trees with the hobgoblin. "Wait up you two!" I whisper-shouted. "You're gonna get lost."

More accurately, *I* was going to get lost if they left me behind.

They never seemed to get lost.

We plunged into the dense tree line and were suddenly enveloped in an all-encompassing fog. It rose high above my head, cutting off my vision of everything lower than fifteen feet above us.

In the distance, the heavy sound of footsteps thundered slowly but steadily closer. I couldn't help wondering what we were hearing. It sounded like a dinosaur. But I was pretty sure there were no dinosaurs in Enchanted.

Were there?

The mist swayed and Sebille's face appeared out of it. Too close. I yelped before I could stop myself. The thunderous footsteps stopped.

Sebille smacked a hand over my mouth. My eyes went as wide as golf balls over the barrier of her fingers. Sebille jerked her head and turned away. I fell in behind her, praying she didn't get too far away from me.

I wondered if she'd let me stick my hand into the neckline of her dress to hold on.

Nope. She'd kill me outright.

Maybe we could tie our wrists together with one of her socks. Goddess knew they were long enough. They rose up her bony thighs like really ugly support stockings.

As if she'd heard me dissing her socks, Sebille turned a glare on me.

Or, maybe that was just her face. Sebille suffered from RBF.

Resting Barracuda Face.

Said barracuda face jerked toward a light in the

distance. I had no idea what it was, but if it was inside, it had to be better than the mist-strangled woods. I nodded.

Behind us, thunder rolled, and I was pretty sure it wasn't a storm.

The bone juddering sound had the cadence of slow, steady footfalls, morphed by the mist. And they appeared to be gaining on us.

A soft buzzing sound was the only warning I got. Sadie shot out of the cloaking mist right at my face. I ducked but managed not to yelp as she braked to a stop in the air in front of me. She started chittering again, occasionally rising above my head and shooting away a few feet in the direction from which we'd come.

I didn't need to understand her. I'd noted the occasional loud cracking sounds behind us too. Trees breaking. As if something really big was making its way through the woods.

I rubbed my chest, wishing I had a giant bottle of that nasty pink stuff that kills stomach acid. Of all the things I'd packed into the canvas backpack, I'd never considered that was something I'd need.

"She says the monster's gaining on us. We need to veer away from our current trajectory until it passes," Sebille whispered.

I liked her thought process because it suggested the thing wasn't actually following us, but just happened to be heading our way. I nodded. "Should we just turn right?"

Sadie said something and shot away from us.

"We'll follow her."

"I hate to sound like a doubter," I told the sprite. "But how do we know she has any better idea where she's going than we do?"

Sebille shrugged. "She grew up in a rain forest. Plus, she can see through the mist. Can you?"

I grimaced. She had a point.

Sebille nodded. "I can't either. Let's keep following her until it doesn't make sense to follow her anymore."

I couldn't argue with that logic. So Sebille and I turned to follow the tiny dragon through the foggy woods. After a while, I realized I could see Sadie's bright form through the mist ahead of us. The fog was thinning.

And my indigestion was better.

Things were looking up.

16

MONSTRUM TEMPESTAS

*A*head of us, rising out of the mist, was a small house. A cabin really, its walls crafted from thick, rough logs that looked as if they'd been shoved together into some semblance of a rectangle by a giant's clumsy hand.

The front wall contained a plain wood door and a single window, which was lit from behind in a welcoming golden light.

Sadie headed for the home. Her flight pattern was jerky and uneven as she continually stopped and looked behind us to the woods, where the sound of crashing trees and footfalls had sped.

The thing behind us was so close I imagined I could feel the heat of its foul breath against my neck as we ran. My legs burning with exhaustion, I sucked heavy, wet air into my lungs and wheezed, my skin oily with fear sweat.

Sadie chittered manically, clearly concerned about the thing on our heels.

I couldn't say I blamed her. Whatever it was, the ground shook beneath the weight of its quickening footsteps and the mist was blown away from it, swirling around us as if set into motion by an enormous fan.

I flew past a massive tree, the trunk so dense and meaty I doubted even Theo the giant could touch his fingertips on the other side if he wrapped his arms around it.

Another thundering footfall sent the leaves and branches high above our heads into motion and foul air gusted past, blowing my hair forward as if I had a wind tunnel at my back.

The stench of the thing was overwhelming. Having only a limited library of scents to compare it to, I nonetheless had some pretty foul comparisons in my memory banks.

The fishy, black magic, rotting flesh miasma that was the monster on our heels was beyond anything I'd ever smelled. Or tasted. The scent was so pervasive, it coated the back of my tongue and painted my airways until it embraced my entire existence in foulness.

The little cabin above the mist loomed ahead. Too far. It's cheerful light an impossible beacon as the mist thickened and embalmed us in its cold, moist embrace.

My lungs screamed. My legs burned. The heavy pack slammed against my back and dug into my shoulders with every step. And still I ran on, knowing that if I stopped...slowed even a little bit... the thing that was stalking us would wrap itself around me and I'd be gone.

An unearthly screech went up behind us, followed by the terrifying sound of wood twisting against wood.

With a final, almost human scream of pain and death, the massive tree I'd passed only a moment before, rose up into the air, roots dripping dirt and something that shimmered silver and liquid in the low light. It hung there, a stark, silent threat. Staring up at it in horror, I tried to see beyond the fog to whatever held the tree. There was nothing. Only the wispy strings of mist rising along its corpse.

The tree suddenly snapped forward, cutting the mist in its flight directly toward me. For just a moment, a tiny beat in time, I saw malevolent dark eyes and a wide mouth filled with several rows of razor-sharp teeth.

"Incoming!" I screamed, dodging sideways in the hopes that the giant missile would somehow miss me when it landed.

No such luck.

Just before it crashed to the ground and skidded toward the cabin, the sharp, biting arms and fingers of its dying branches clawed across my skin and slashed against my legs to send me flying.

My shoulders were wrenched painfully backward as the pack was ripped away from me, caught on one of the branches.

I hit the ground several yards away from the cabin, whose door stood open in silent welcome. Shoving aside the pain crawling over every inch of my body, I pushed to my feet and dove for the door.

Ahead of me, Wicked and Sebille followed the tiny dragon through the opening. Slimy had gone very still in my pocket. I was terrified I might have landed on him when I was thrown. I reached in, finding him soft and still. "Slimy?"

I'm alive. His tone was hushed, trembling with fear.

Fighting guilt for nearly landing on him again, I took a deep breath and relief flared. But it was short-lived. A blur of movement had me turning to find enormous blue eyes staring up at me.

Hobs opened his mouth to speak as another tree died a screeching death behind us. When it was thrown, it created a gentle soughing on the air that sounded innocuous in the deadly fog.

And I knew in that moment I wouldn't be able to escape.

I was tired. Banged up. And my reaction time was too slow. Still, I leaned forward on my toes and tightened my muscles to run.

Hobs' long-fingered hand wrapped around my arm and he screamed, "Hold on, Miss!"

Then the tree crashed into the dirt behind us and something stabbed me between my shoulder blades.

And the world was ripped away from me as everything whirled past at an impossible speed.

My feet touched the ground again and a door slammed behind me. I turned in a daze, just in time to see the inside of the plain wood door ease away, leaving only empty darkness.

The cabin was gone.

My pack with all my comforting goodies was gone too. I took a deep breath and expelled it, telling myself not to focus on the things I couldn't control.

My heart pounding, I took a moment to get my bearings. The air smelled fresh. Well, by comparison. There was a pervasive stench of ozone, as if a violent storm hovered on the horizon.

I turned to find Hobs standing next to me, his small chest heaving. When he saw me looking, he shook his head. "That was a close one, Miss."

I couldn't disagree. I gave him a quick hug. "Thanks, buddy."

Glancing around, I saw my friends ahead, still following the dragon. But something was wrong. I rubbed my chest despite the fact there was no pain. No burning.

Just a lingering memory of an ache I no longer felt.

Shaking it off, I started after the small group, wondering why I couldn't shake the sense that we were heading the wrong way.

Then I remembered Archie's words as he'd stabbed a finger against his own chest. *It will be here. This is your magic to call, Sorceress. Embrace it, infuse it into your cells. It's every bit as much a part of your strength as your domination of the artifact library is.*

I stopped, his words reverberating through my mind. Repeating and repeating until I understood what he'd been telling me.

I turned to my right and waited. Nothing. I made another quarter turn, facing the direction from which we'd just come and secretly praying that wasn't the right direction. Nothing. I turned again, pain burned in my chest.

"Stop!" I called out to my friends.

Sebille turned to me. Sadie jerked to a stop in front of her.

"Meow," said my cat, who, in normal Wicked fashion, was where he needed to be, down by my feet.

"What's wrong?" Sebille asked.

I pointed. "We need to go this way."

The sprite looked as if she was thinking about arguing. But she must have remembered Archie's words too. She simply inclined her head and angled toward me.

And we started off again through the dark.

The going was slow. The ground was oddly spongy and clung to my feet with every step. My legs were burning and I was covered in sweat. The mist was gone. I was happy about that, but the place where we found ourselves was warm and airless, the sky above lit with an odd ambient light. By the time we'd walked what felt like ten miles but which was probably only one, my whole body was slimy and my legs were shaking.

I glanced at Sebille. Sadie was asleep on her shoulder and Sebille had one hand resting gently on the little dragon, a tender gesture that made my heart warm. The sprite didn't seem to be struggling as much as I was, but she was clearly tired. She'd stumbled more than once in the last few minutes.

"Do you want me to carry your pack?" I asked.

She shook her head.

"You should shift into your sprite form," I told her. Flying would be easier than walking on the spongy ground.

My assistant slid a gaze to me. Something that looked like warmth filled her eerie green gaze. She flipped a hand into the air. "This atmosphere is anti-aeronautical. The heavy, wet air weighs wings down. Believe it or not, flying would be worse."

That would explain why Sadie was curled up on Sebille's shoulder instead of flitting around as she'd done before.

I nodded, wishing we'd reach the tear soon so we could fix it and get back home. Maybe conversation would make the time go faster. "I wonder how the guys are doing against the monster."

Sebille frowned. "I'm a little worried about that. After seeing...or not seeing...that last monster, I'm realizing there are much worse things than what we've already experienced that could slip through that breach."

I'd had the same thought. "What was that thing?"

Sebille shook her head. "No idea."

A soft breeze slid over my skin. It was the same temperature as the air around us, but it bathed the sweat coating my skin and cooled me just the same. I closed my eyes and sighed. "That feels wonderful."

Sebille didn't respond.

I opened my eyes and looked at her. She was staring straight ahead, her gaze unfocused. She seemed lost in thought. "Something wrong?"

She shook off the glazed expression and frowned over at me. "I don't know. I've just been sensing something the last few minutes. Something feels...wrong."

Another cooling breeze lifted my hair. But, with Sebille's words sending a chill down my spine, I didn't enjoy it nearly as much.

My pocket juddered, and I looked down as a small green head appeared above the edge. *She's right*, Slimy said. *It's probably coming from that glowing yellow ball over there.*

"Where?" Sebille and I asked at the same time. I did a one-hundred-and-eighty-degree scan of the area ahead of us, as far as I could see anyway, and saw nothing but semi-opaque darkness. Judging by the sprite's confused expression, I figured she'd had the same result.

But the frog knows what the frog knows.

Wind gusted past, bringing with it a heavier scent of ozone. Like the air smells just before the sky opens up and dumps cats and dogs on your head.

I pulled Slimy out of my pocket and held him up so he could see better. "Are we heading right for it?" I asked him.

No.

I relaxed a bit.

It's heading right for us. Run! he screamed, his usual superior tone gone in a moment of panic.

I turned to the side, thinking a change of direction would be good, and started to run. Sebille had the same idea. She turned toward me. We smacked in the middle and went down. The dragon lifted off Sebille's shoulder with a squawk of outrage. All I saw of Slimy was his pudgy green form somersaulting through the air.

Sebille and I shot back to our feet. "Pick a direction," I screamed, wind whipping my hair around my face.

She pointed past me. I pointed past her.

It was like a deadly game of rock, paper scissors in Hades.

Debris spun past on a gust of moist air. I ducked to keep from being knocked over by a tree branch as thick as my arm.

I scooped Slimy up and tucked him into my pocket. Spotting Wicked staring into the face of the wind, I grabbed him too, holding him close as the wind pummeled us.

He yowled unhappily but didn't try to get away from me.

The next blast of wind literally pulled me off the ground. For just a beat, the bottoms of my sneakers hovered an inch above the spongy surface. "We need to find shelter from this storm!" I yelled into Sebille's face.

She nodded. We both looked back the way we'd come, but there was no cheerful little cabin to offer us protection.

In fact, there was nothing anywhere. Except a small copse of trees to our left. After the last experience in the woods of the abyss. I wasn't in a hurry to enter another one.

Another gust seemed to blow Hobs at us. He flew through the air and smacked up hard against my hip, wrapping his arms around my leg as the wind tried to tug him away from me.

Sadie was airborne again, her tiny wings braced against the onslaught of the driving wind. She was chittering wildly, her eyes flashing different colors with every throb of her wings. Sebille nodded. "Okay." She looked at me. "Sadie says it's nearly on top of us. We need to disrupt it, or it's going to spin us into its vortex."

"Vortex?" I shoved hair out of my face, screaming into the wind.

Sebille turned and pointed.

There was movement in the dark. Several things spinning. I realized it was a dozen or so small twisters, arrayed in a circle and throwing up debris like tires throwing water off a highway.

I'd never seen anything like it. "What in the thirteen worlds is that?" I asked the sprite.

"An outer perimeter," she screamed back, pointing into the sky.

I looked where she was pointing and nearly swallowed my tongue.

The thing was massive. The size of a large building and taller than the tallest skyscraper I'd ever seen. Its "head" was a series of updrafts that swirled and snapped above it. It had no face that I could see, though every once in a while two, large dark holes would appear in the form of eyes, lightning snapping at their center.

"*Monstrum Tempestas*," Sebille said.

"Storm monster?" I repeated, frowning. "You've got to be kidding me."

The eyes appeared again, flaring wide as twin bolts of lightning flashed from their depths and speared the ground mere feet away.

The air became supercharged, thickening and exploding outward to slam into us. I was blasted into the air and landed half a block away, the spongy earth taking some of the sting out of the violence of my landing.

Two more bolts slammed into the sponge, sending it into the air in large chunks that battered us as we tried to climb to our feet.

I covered Wicked as best I could, while keeping the pocket holding the frog away from the maelstrom. Sebille crawled over to me, pointing to the small group of trees huddled against the storm. I nodded and we climbed to our feet, heads down, and ran as fast as we could toward the only shelter we could find.

The storm monster's violence was softened within the woods. Though flying branches and ominously creaking trees became an issue. But the relative safety gave us a moment to take stock and make a plan.

Best laid plans and all that. The goddess was having a good laugh on us. We never got past the taking stock part. Because we realized we'd somehow lost Sadie. And when we found her, that was when fear and worry turned to terror.

17

LATER NAIDER

*T*he little dragon's scales had turned a bright, eye-piercing yellow that flashed warning into the darkness swirling around her. Despite the brutality of the wind battering against her, Sadie's wings thrummed lazily on the air, seemingly unaffected.

Sebille started forward on a fear-filled cry, but I stopped her with a hand on her arm. Something about the little dragon's calm presence facing off against the monster told me she was all right. I pointed to the illuminated sphere around the dragon. "Look. Where her yellow light is touching the storm, the wind has settled."

Sebille gave up tugging to be free. "She's so little. There's no way she won't be killed."

I was shocked to see a single, silvery tear sliding

down Sebille's freckled cheek. I wrapped an arm around her shoulders. And she promptly shook it off.

I sighed, fighting a grin. Some things never changed. Sebille didn't do compassion. She saw it as pity. And, to the sprite, pity was a monster as ugly as the thing we were facing.

I would have to speak to her in her own language. "Suck it up, buttercup," I said. "The dragon's a lot more than she appears. Kanish told us that, remember? And, judging from what I'm seeing, Kanish was right. She's holding that storm back with her little yellow light."

Sebille's jaw tightened until I was surprised her teeth didn't break. But she slowly nodded, awarding me the point.

Despite my hard words, I wasn't one-hundred-percent sold on the whole "small but mighty" shtick the half-feral dragon had given us. So I looked at Hobs, jerking my chin slightly, and he nodded, disappearing in a blur of movement.

He reappeared just behind Sadie, ready to grab her and get the heck out of Dodge with her if it looked as if things were about to go bad.

I was pleased to see that the area of yellow light had grown enough to encompass Hobs, standing behind and below the dragon. And half of the smaller whirlwinds were gone.

Still, lightning flared from the monster's eyes, shearing through the night sky to slam into the trees where we hid.

It thought to distract Sadie by putting us in danger. A good strategy, but not one that we were going to let it win. "We need to keep moving," I told Sebille. "One strike could take us all out right now."

Understanding lit her gaze and she nodded.

"No matter what happens, don't scream," I said. "Don't distract Sadie. She's beating it back."

Sebille grabbed my hand as I started to melt into the trees. "If something happens to me, you can do it, Naida. You can close that breach. You've always had that power inside you. It's just that nobody ever taught you how to pull it out and use it. You did that yourself."

I stared at her for a long moment. That was the longest pep talk the sprite had ever given. It could very well be the *only* pep talk the sprite had ever given. Finally, I nodded. "If something happens to me..."

She shook her head. "Not an option. Later, Naider." She popped into her sprite form and buzzed away before I could respond.

I barked out a laugh, shaking my head. *Later Naider.* Then I settled Wicked to the ground and patted my pocket. "Let's go, troops."

We'd barely gone twenty steps before a bolt of

lightning seared through the trees and obliterated the area surrounding Sebille.

When the too-bright electrical light flashed away, the trees were on fire, smoke slowly rising from the crater left behind in the ground, and there was no Sebille.

She was gone.

Obliterated in the flare of a single lightning bolt.

Understanding speared the center of my chest like a deadly blade. Agony tore at my fragile heart, ripping it to shreds in a moment of world-altering clarity. I slapped a hand over my mouth and held my scream of pain behind it. Tears overflowed my eyes and dripped over the restraining hand.

Wicked trotted forward several steps, his mouth open on a plaintive yowl.

The sound sent me to my knees.

We need to keep moving, the frog said, his voice muffled and sad.

I shook my head. "Sebille," I whispered, sniffling as her loss ripped through my chest and gut, leaving me emotionally hemorrhaging and shaking.

Flames ate along the broken trees, the fire hungry and fierce. Thick, gray smoke rose from the wood it ravaged.

Nothing could have survived that strike.

I coughed as the first tendrils of smoke found me, wrapping around me and invading my nose, stinging my eyes.

Wicked slowly turned back, trotting purposefully in my direction. "Meow," he said.

I shook my head, scraping at my tears.

"Meow!" he repeated, slashing at me with a claw.

I barely noticed the pain of his reprimand. But I shoved to my feet, recognizing I still had a job to do. People's lives rested on my shoulders.

I turned away and started trudging toward the open sky I could see in the distance. Once we'd gotten around the monstrous storm, I'd realign myself in the right direction.

After that...

My emotions were too raw, my thoughts too chaotic to decide what I'd do after that. One thing at a time. One foot in front of the other.

No thinking. Only moving.

We circled around the storm monster, my gaze locked on the slowly receding vertical wind tunnel. Its entire front half was bathed in golden light, like sunshine, and the light seemed to be making the monster shrink.

But it was still a long way from gone, and I wondered how much longer Sadie could hold her magic to keep it back.

Then I realized the dragon was no longer there. Did Hobs have her? And if he did...

A fresh round of lightning bolts speared the night, slamming in brutal jabs into the trees that had formerly protected us.

The light show continued until the whole line of trees was reduced to fiery vertical wicks lighting the sky. Like giant candles on a spongy deathday cake.

The thought caught me unawares, ripping the air from my lungs and making me double over and retch onto the ground. I threw up until I had nothing left for my stomach to reject, a fresh spate of tears painting my heated cheeks.

The air next to me shifted, and a long-fingered hand found my shoulder. "Miss?"

I ran my sleeve over my mouth and sniffled. "Hobs. I'm glad you're safe."

Little Sadie rose up from his shoulder and hung on the air, chittering excitedly. I figured she was probably recounting her amazing control over the storm monster, proud of herself as she had a right to be. I forced a smile, touching her tiny snout with a gentle finger. "You did really well," Sadie girl. "Really, really well."

Her eyes turned a happy pink, and her snout opened in a smile. But then she looked around, a question transforming her expressive face.

I stiffened, realizing I was going to have to tell her about Sebille. But I couldn't. Meeting Hobs' eyes briefly, I saw the moment when he understood, and my stomach tightened again. I shoved the nausea back. I needed to take the same advice I'd given Sebille. I needed to "suck it up, buttercup". "We separated," I told the little dragon. "She'll meet up with us later."

Hobs' expressive blue eyes glistened with tears that fell silently down his cheeks. I wrapped an arm around him and pulled him close, a quick hug to let him know I understood. But we couldn't wallow yet. There would be time for grieving later. "Let's go," I told them, rubbing the burning spot on my sternum. "I see the fissure ahead."

And I realized I did see it. I'd been seeing it for a while, but my mind hadn't recognized it until just that moment. With a final glance back at the engulfed copse of trees where my friend had died, I pushed my grief to the back of my mind, to be pulled out when the lives of so many people didn't hang in the balance.

The fracture hung in the sky in the distance. It was shaped like an elongated pear and sent silvery light into the night. There was movement in the tear, frantic and violent. As if I were seeing bits and pieces of the battle going on inside Croakies at that very moment.

Please goddess, don't let that be it.

Just the thought of the havoc being wreaked and Rustin and Grym in the thick of it made me sick again. I couldn't lose another friend.

I couldn't...

I swallowed hard, the knot in my throat joining the twisting pain in my belly. I was a mess. And depression made my limbs feel so heavy I could barely move them. But I slogged forward, the odd rip in the sky calling me to it like a beacon.

The burning sensation I'd been feeling in my chest hadn't lessened. In fact, as I drew nearer the fracture, it had gotten worse. So much worse. It was one of those times I really wished I had healing energies to call.

Sebille had had healing energies.

I shoved the thought away, knowing that way lay a depression so severe I could barely breathe just from letting my mind drift in that direction.

Instead, I focused on the horizon ahead, Hobs and Sadie were keeping an eye on our perimeter. Sadie flew a wide circle around us, her happy colors like a beacon in the near distance. Hobs shot ahead every few minutes, scouting out the area we were approaching and filling me in on anything we needed to worry about.

Fortunately, there hadn't been much. But Hobs' most recent expedition was lasting too long. To the point that I was starting to worry about him.

I tried to hail Sadie, but she was dancing around the perimeter, her soft, happy chirping a comforting sound in the near distance.

I looked down at Wicked. "Do you sense Hobs nearby?"

My cat looked up, his eyes round and glowing orange, which told me he was using his prodigious magical energy to read the area around us.

"Meow." I took his quiet tone to be a negative. Though I knew it was partially because of Sebille. The sprite had pretended to hate the cat. And he'd sucked up to her just to annoy her. But I knew, deep down, the two had grown fond of each other during the time Mr. Wicked had been with us.

Slimy was quiet in my pocket. As an excuse to nudge him out of his depression, I reached in and pulled him out, holding him in front of my nose. "Hey," I said.

The frog blinked slowly. *Hey.*

"You okay?" I asked.

His squishy form rippled in a froggy shrug.

"It will be okay," I told him.

He sighed. *She was always snarky to me, but I kind of enjoyed verbally sparring with her.*

I forced a grin. "Ooh, look at you, Mr. Five-dollar words."

He chuckled.

"Do you see anything ahead that concerns you? Hobs hasn't come back from his latest scouting expedition."

I held the frog up and waited for him to read the

energies on the air. *Nothing. Except for that giant hole in the sky.*

"Yeah," I told him. "That's our target. What do you think of it?"

I felt him frown in my mind. *What do you mean?*

"What kind of energy is the hole giving off?"

It's pretty neutral, really. Nothing offensive. It doesn't feel dangerous.

"That's good," I told him.

We fell silent. Me dropping into my thoughts of closing the fissure and Slimy thinking...who knew what? He could be dreaming about eating calcium-coated crickets for all I knew.

Blech!

An hour later, I stopped at the end of a street that started from nowhere and ended in nothing about a quarter-mile away. The virtual street was lined on both sides by buildings, mostly brick. They were all low-slung and blocky, looking as if they'd been built around the same time by the same builder. It was a pretty spot, the buildings created of several different but complementary hues of formed bricks and stone. And I recognized the face of each and every one of them. Especially the building on the right, dead center of the street.

Croakies.

It was my neighborhood.

I scanned the area, looking for Hobs. I didn't see him.

My gaze slid to the familiar scratched sign with the ugly frog, which hung in front of my store. Was that where he'd be? Was he waiting for us?

No. Hobs wouldn't do that. He'd know I'd be worried. If he didn't come back to me, it was because he couldn't. He was hurt. Or...

I swallowed bile and pulled air into my lungs. I wasn't going there.

Impatient with my dithering at the end of the street, Sadie flashed past me, her small form a bright and happy mote sliding through the darkness. I stepped off of the spongy ground onto the asphalt of fake-Enchanted, wishing it were Enchanted for real. Wishing we'd never come into the abyss. Wishing... well, just wishing.

I put one foot in front of the other until I started to feel more confident. The street was quiet. Nothing moved except the amalgamate dragon, me, and my cat.

My steps sped. The sooner I closed the fissure, the sooner I could get home, and the sooner we could start to heal.

I thought of Queen Sindra, and my heart clenched. I'd have to tell her about Sebille. The thought stopped me in my tracks. What was I doing? Nothing was going to be right again. Ever. And if Hobs was lost to me too...

I suddenly couldn't stand it. "Hobs!" My scream echoed down the street, pulsing away from me in concentric circles of slowly ebbing sound. When it hit the buildings, my voice died, slashed into silence by two rows of fake brick in a faux existence.

But Hobs didn't come.

He didn't come.

Tears burned in my eyes. I fought them. And then I saw something that sent the tears away. A small form, dressed in white, with a long, red, and green knitted scarf around his neck.

Hobs!

The hobgoblin stood in the middle of the street, staring silently in my direction but not speaking. I started to walk toward him, my footsteps getting fast and faster as I grew close. Impatience soon had me running. I was only vaguely aware of Mr. Wicked yowling at me. I wouldn't have noticed the cat at all except for the tracks of bleeding slashes he put along my calf. But that pain slowly broke through my impatient rush, and I slid to a stop.

Wicked rubbed his head over my leg and purred. Loud enough to reverberate along the empty street.

Hobs stood silent. His skinny limbs straight and unmoving.

"Hobs?" I asked.

But even as I said his name, I knew it wasn't him.

The footsteps were a soft cadence against the road. Growing louder by the moment. They echoed to the buildings as my voice had, and then died.

The two men approached unhurriedly. As if the

walkers knew they had me right where they wanted me. And all I could do was wait.

I knew who they were. And I knew in my writhing gut that they had Hobs.

And I was going to get him back if it killed me, along with both of the evil wizards walking slowly toward me down the street.

AND AFTER THAT?

"We knew you'd come. Eventually," the taller one said. The one called George.

The other wizard nodded, his grin showing teeth that had been sharpened to points in the front. Like a vampire's.

I fought a shudder. "Give me back my friend."

George laughed. It wasn't a comforting sound. "You banish us to the abyss, and now you're making demands?" He shook his dark head, the hair looking greasy under the light of the fissure above us.

I shrugged, trying to look unconcerned. "To be fair, you guys attacked us first. We were just defending ourselves."

George cocked his head. "That's not how we see it, Sorceress."

"You know who I am." It wasn't a question. He

clearly recognized me.

"I always make a point to know who I'm killing." His teeth weren't sharpened, but they didn't need to be. The eyes above them were like the dead of winter. Icy with deadly intent. "That's just good business."

The wizards lifted their hands, squeezing them into fists which they lifted to chest height, folded fingers pointing toward the street. Black, oily energy surrounded their fists and ran up their arms and into their faces through bulging black veining under the surface of their skin. The veining spread across the wizards' cheeks, branched over their filth-covered necks, and disappeared into their hairlines.

George's gaze locked onto mine, he allowed his hatred to throb within the glossy black depths as the two men opened their fists and let their magic run in liquid rivulets to the street.

I watched the magic puddle on the asphalt, wondering what the effects would be, and then jumped in surprise and fear as the asphalt cracked loudly beneath the wizards' ugly energy. The midnight-colored liquid continued to run from their hands, gathering in the growing cracks that had continued to spread until we were forced to back-track or risk having the energy touch us.

Wicked shot away from me, heading toward the sidewalk and moving quickly along the buildings, invisible unless you knew he was there.

The asphalt buckled under my feet and I lost my balance, my arms windmilling as I tried to keep from falling forward.

It buckled again, more violently, and the black liquid boiled up out of the cracks and splashed against my shoes.

I immediately felt the heat of that magic. I smelled the canvas of my sneakers burning as it ate its way through my shoes like acid.

I gave a sharp little scream of fear and started to run, following Wicked's path toward the sidewalk.

The street broke again, cutting me off in a quickly widening river of oily dark magic that smelled like sulfur and was hot enough to turn my skin red even from a distance. I spun on my heel and started running the other way, determined to beat the magic to the other side.

George threw a hand into the air in a fist, and the black liquid ran from his ears. From his nose and mouth, flowing down his long body in a film that washed away his humanity as it flowed, leaving behind only the liquid rush of the acidic energy.

Without another word, the two wizards melted into the fissures, their magic so condensed and powerful it ate the street where it touched and flowed faster than I could run away. The ugly river sliced off my retreat, threatening to strand me in a small island of asphalt at the center of the street.

But I had no intention of letting myself get

trapped. Even if it meant my death, I was going to try to make it to that sidewalk. I dug in, racing the glossy death that was rushing toward me and knowing even as I ran that I would lose.

At the boiling edge of the newly formed river of sulfurous energy, I leaped, praying to the goddess that I could make it to the sidewalk beyond the toxic liquid.

I knew the moment my feet left the ground that I was doomed.

As I plunged downward, my shoes inches away from hitting the acidic river, I heard the soft throb of wings on the air behind me. I mentally prepared for the agony of the river's touch, hoping I could take one step in the center and then leap out again, minimizing the damage to my legs.

But my sneakers never hit the poisonous energy. At the last possible moment, massive clawed fingers wrapped around my arms and jerked me skyward, lifting me above the buildings into a shimmering night sky. Even as I tried to wrap my mind around the new danger, the claws released my arms and sent me plunging downward, onto a familiar flat roof.

I looked up to see a human-sized dragon with a rainbow-hued body and fading orange eyes. The dragon's wings fluttered several more times and then stuttered as the glow of its eyes was cut off behind its lowering lids.

Sadie?

The dragon seemed to lose consciousness as she plunged toward the roof where I stood. I realized she was heading directly for me and panicked, glancing quickly around. There wasn't room for a dragon her size to land. If she did, she was going to skid right off the side of the roof and into the nasty black river below.

I was going to have to catch her. She'd probably flatten me. But I had no choice. I danced sideways, my arms outstretched, and then adjusted as she came closer, when I realized I was going to miss. I closed my eyes and said a quick prayer.

A soft pop of air had my eyes opening as the dragon spun toward me in her normal size. With a gust of relieved air, I reached out and wrapped my fingers carefully around the little rainbow dragon, pulling her against my body and dropping to my knees with her nestled safely against my belly.

Her heart beat hard and strong against my fingers and she seemed to be breathing okay. I figured she'd just pushed the limits of her magic when she'd grown herself to help me. I owed her big for that. And, if we survived the current mess, I'd spend a lot of time, making sure she knew I was grateful.

"What's going on?" asked the frog in my pocket.

I reached down and tugged him out. "We're safe for the moment." I peered over the edge of the roof and found the river receding, the oily black magic sucking backward and beginning to form back into the wizards' humanoid shapes. "But there's more trouble ahead."

As the wizards reformed, I caught movement across the street and my heartbeat jumped into panic mode. Mr. Wicked was moving along the shadows, a glossy silver mist trailing behind him. As I watched, he encircled the two wizards, the mist settling along the ground in a perfect circle that began to glow as it fell into place.

He'd trapped them in a witch circle. My cat was a genius.

"We need to move. Wicked's bought us some time."

I slipped the frog back into my pocket and pushed to my feet, still clutching the dragon gently against my chest.

I ran toward the door at the center of the roof. At the Croakies in the real world I kept the door locked and warded, but I was praying the Croakies look-alike in the abyss wasn't equally secure.

The knob turned in my hand, and I thanked the goddess, hurrying down the stairs to the landing outside my apartment. I glanced through my open apartment door and saw only swirling blackness. The sight made me shudder. Apparently, the abyss didn't bother with details when it created the likeness of a physical image.

Similarly, the artifact library looked like a mini

void. But I noticed as I descended the stairs, my mind picturing the items that should be there, they popped into view, one by one, slowly populating the enormous space.

The dividing door into the bookstore was already there as I reached the last step and stopped. I stared down at the swirling void, unwilling to step down into nothingness. I couldn't shake the feeling that I would step into a black hole and just keep falling forever.

But as I stared, silvery motes began to dance in the abyss, slowly congealing into a solid mass at the center and then spreading outward to represent the concrete floor of my artifact library.

I carefully lowered one foot and, when I found it solid, allowed my weight to fall onto the foot. I quickly took the few steps toward the door, still feeling like it was all going to melt away and send me plunging into nothingness.

As I reached for the knob, the door started to glow, radiating heat and light like a giant lightbulb. Pain sizzled across my fingers when I touched it.

Frowning, I tugged my sleeve down and, taking a deep breath, quickly grasped the knob through my sleeve. I sucked in air as pain seared through my palm, but I managed to turn the knob and shove it inward before yanking my blistered hand away.

A disconcerting, ethereal glow filled the space beyond the door. Bright enough to burn my eyes, the space looked like I imagined an Angel in Heaven would look. Pure, unformed light with an underlying impression of gentle movement.

It was as unending an effect of nothingness as the black of the abyss, but it was pure light, where the abyss was its opposite. A complete lack of light.

I instinctively knew as I stood there, unsure whether to move into it or walk away, that I'd found the fissure in the abyss I'd been looking for.

I took a deep breath and tried to calm my nerves so I could do what needed to be done. It wasn't easy. The recent battle in the street and my concern for my friends had kept my heart pretty much pounding like a bass drum for the last couple of hours.

But I needed to calm myself before I could tug my magic forward and heal the breach.

I closed my eyes, breathing slowly and in as controlled a manner as I could manage. With my eyes closed, I noticed how hot the breach was. The heat pulsed against my skin as its impossible light burned through my lids, removing the sense of darkness even there.

Tiny stars danced against my retinas from the light. It was impossible to block it out to find the soothing darkness I needed.

Slimy wriggled inside my pocket. I tried to ignore him but found myself waiting for every movement, focusing hard on what he was doing. Until I was pretty sure I could feel the slow bulge and retraction of his throat as he breathed.

I shook my head, taking a long, deep breath and expelling it slowly in another attempt to center myself.

The breach tugged at me, slithered over my skin, and called to me with an oily voice.

No, that wasn't the breach talking. Breaches didn't talk.

My pulse shot skyward again as the bright white of the fissure split apart and an enraged wizard reached through it to clasp a brutal hand around my throat, yanking me into the breach.

I yelped once before George's vicious grip cut off my air supply. He dragged me up against his body and growled in my face, rage painting his gaze with swirling energy.

Despite my surprised terror, I noticed two things. One, the light was gone. And two, we were standing inside the bookstore, with bookshelves and everything.

For one terrifying beat, I thought the wizard had pulled me through the breach. Which would mean that he'd gone through the breach himself. My stomach twisted on that new fear. What if the wizards recognized the breach for what it was? What if they went through? Rustin and Grym weren't prepared for their kind of inhuman, lethal energy.

I shoved the fear aside. I couldn't let it happen. I

had to defeat them before they noticed the open door leading to freedom.

But how?

I glanced around for anything I could use to fight them. The bookstore was empty of useful artifacts. The world beyond the window was black and unformed.

I was coming to understand that the void only spent energy replicating things that were needed in that moment. Anything outside that need was just void.

I clawed at George's murderous hold on my throat, fighting to pull air into my lungs and hearing the bones in my neck grinding ominously underneath his crushing grip.

"You stupid magic jockey!" he screamed, flinging me away to crash against one of the bookshelves. The impact sent several heavy volumes crashing down onto my choking form. I heaved in a painful breath, coughing on the acidic air as if my throat was burned and tender.

I looked at my hands and realized I'd dropped Sadie at some point. My eyes slid around the space, looking for the little dragon. I didn't see her. But I did notice the dividing door.

Closed. With a white light glowing through the cracks between the door and the frame.

The breach apparently lived on whichever side of the door I didn't inhabit.

George lifted his fist and said something in Latin, which I didn't catch. My blood ran cold as the oily black magic flowed down his arm again.

I'd have a lot harder time avoiding the flesh-eating magic in that room. I had no place to go.

The outside door slammed open and my world crashed.

The other wizard walked in with a mean grin on his ugly face. He held a magically crafted cage, comprised of the black energy that was the wizard's specialty. My cat was inside the cage, hissing and spitting and trying to claw the evil creature through the sulfurous black bars.

Wicked?

My cat's gaze caught mine and he calmed. Sitting on his haunches, his orange gaze held mine as his sigil began to glow.

I gave him a tiny nod.

In two long strides, George grabbed my arm and lifted me in the air, the black magic dripping down his other fist, mere inches from my face. "You're not getting away from us this time."

I forced myself not to look at the deadly energy so near my skin. Instead, I reached up and slapped a hand against his temple, sending everything I had into his beady little brain.

Silvery energy flared outward, unfocused and rabid, and had nowhere to go except through his skin and into his skull.

George stiffened under the onslaught, his long body convulsing under the infusion of what should be only collective magics, used for calling things to me, magical things, and keeping them under my thumb. But with Wicked helping the magic focus, and given that it had only one place to go, my generally harmless magic had gained legs.

George's eyes rolled back in his head, showing me only the blood-shot whites, and the magic he'd been calling to hurt me slid back inside his skin. His knees buckled and he lost his grip on my arm as he folded toward the floor.

"You witch!" the other wizard screamed. Before I could react, he shot a bolt of sulfurous magic into my chest. It punched me like a fist, so powerful it shot me backward and into the air. I hit my head when I crashed against the shelves and the world turned charcoal as I started to pass out.

I didn't quite fall unconscious. I was dimly aware of a ruckus beyond my charcoal world.

A bolt of pure energy sizzled past, hot and angry. It had passed close enough to burn my ear and turn the books behind me to dust and chunks.

I fought the oblivion that was trying to tug me down, and opened my eyes.

At first, I thought I was seeing double. Two dragons were battling the wizard.

Or where they dragonflies?

So pretty.

A blur on the air made my eyes go crossed. And a soft warmth tucked itself into my belly with a comforting rumble.

Slowly. Ever so slowly. I climbed out of the haziness that had been holding me down, and my thoughts cleared. I placed a hand on my cat, who was purring as he used his centering energies to bring me back. And I glanced up into the worried blue eyes of Hobs, who, I realized, was cradling my head in his lap. "Oh good. You're safe," I said to them. The words were stupid. So inadequate. But the emotion they couldn't adequately portray blossomed like a prize-winning rose in my heart.

"Miss Sebille found me. She saved me from the wizard's trap," Hobs told me.

I grimaced. I'd heard of those. They were comprised of the burning magic they'd used against Wicked and me in the street. Unfortunately, the prisoner couldn't avoid touching it, because it was infused into every bar of the prison.

I realized with horror that Wicked had been in a prison of the same type.

I shoved upright just in time to see a combined blast of green energy from Sebille and Sadie send the remaining wizard flying through the door, into the void beyond.

A moment later, George's body lifted off the floor on a blanket of sprite energy and followed the other wizard out.

Then Sebille swung her hand to slam the door closed, and I watched in dazed pleasure as a complex ward settled over the lock to keep them out.

I leaned against the bookshelves behind me and sighed. My body was one giant ache. "I thought I'd gotten rid of you," I told the sprite.

She grinned, as I'd hoped she would. "Nope. You're still stuck with me." She held up her thumb and finger, showing a tiny space between them and said, "That lightning missed me by this much."

I grinned as tears burned my eyes. "Thanks." I wasn't entirely sure if I was thanking her for surviving, or for coming to my rescue. Again. But it didn't matter. She simply nodded, her own eyes suspiciously bright.

Hobs jumped to his feet. "Miss, if you don't mind, I'd like to go home now."

I opened my mouth to respond but couldn't speak because I started to laugh. My laughter quickly turned hysterical as all the emotions that had been riding me since entering the abyss swamped me in a wash that turned me to mush.

Sebille laughed with me, clearly ready for the nightmare to end too.

Hobs looked worried for our sanity.

I slowly pushed to my feet, wiping tears from my eyes, and took his hand. "Yeah," I said, slightly breathless. "Going home sounds really good."

19

I'M FEELING BETTER ABOUT IT

*A*s it had in Plex, my magic worked differently in the void than at home. It was stronger, more robust than usual, which made doing what I needed to do so much easier than it could have been.

And it also made it harder.

One of the things Archie had warned me about was overflowing the system. "It's a delicate balance," he'd told me. "If you're too heavy-handed with the fix, you risk creating new tears in the tissue of the void."

I'd swallowed hard at that information, knowing my limitations so painfully well.

Standing in front of the dividing door, I stared at the glow escaping around the frame and wiped my sweaty palms over my jeans.

"Is there a problem?" the sprite asked.

Remembering how sad I'd been when I'd thought she was gone, I bit back a snarky response. She'd grown up with her magic, surrounded by Fae who helped her understand her limits and her strengths. I hadn't had that luxury. I tried not to think about my early years without my magic. They were years during which something boiled and spit deep inside me, yet I'd had no idea what it was.

It had been terrifying and unsettling.

I hadn't known why I was always feeling restless. I hadn't understood why I'd felt as if something was missing. And I hadn't wanted to talk about it to anyone for fear I'd be cast out on my own as punishment for not being like everyone around me.

I hadn't even known why I'd felt different until I'd turned eighteen and my magic had slammed into me with the force of a freight train, refusing to be ignored any longer.

I shook off my thoughts, shocked that I'd even had them. I couldn't remember the last time I'd thought about those years. As far as I was concerned, it hadn't been nearly long enough.

"Naida?"

Sebille's voice was soft, her tone gentle. I must have really looked spooked.

I shook my head. "Archie told me not to use too much energy. I have no idea what 'too much' even is."

Sebille nodded. "That's why we brought the

rodent-killer, right?"

She was right. Mr. Wicked was my best tool for focusing my magic. I needed to trust that he would keep me on the right path. I nodded, wiped my palms on my pants again, and took a deep breath.

As if he'd heard us mention his name, Wicked trotted over and sat down in front of me, his warm boohind planted on my shoes.

I closed my eyes, took another deep breath, and then lifted my hands, palms toward the door. I opened my eyes. "I'm ready."

Sebille sent a trickle of green energy toward the overheated knob and tugged, pulling the door into the room.

The bright white light seemed even harsher than it had before. I squinted against it, feeling the energy coiling in my belly as Wicked's sigil started to glow. With Wicked's gentling, the magic slid from its space deep within me and eased slowly toward my hands. When the energy reached the end of my fingers, it stopped, awaiting my invitation to move into the light.

I held it tightly, afraid that if I let it go, it would explode out of control from my body. My experiences with using my keeper magics in other dimensions has been erratic, unpredictable. But, I realized as I took stock of the magic filling me, that I was calm. The magic raged beneath my skin, but it felt focused. All I had to do was trust myself.

That was all I had to do.

Just. Trust.

I allowed the magic to ease from my fingertips. It flowed smoothly away from me, hit the center of the breach and dove into it, spreading out from the insertion point with controlled fingers of silvery energy. I continued to release the energy as I started to see shapes beyond the breach. The hole my magic was creating began in the center and spread, slowly at first and then more rapidly through the blinding white nothingness.

The center grew. I recognized the artifact library of *my* Croakies. Shakespeare's desk appeared and, not too far away, was the standing mirror Sebille and I used to communicate with other supernormals. In the foreground, the steps leading to my apartment slowly eased into view.

When the edges of the white void were no wider than my hand, I started to pull back my magic, easing it to a stop as the last of the breach was nibbled away by the remaining threads of power.

It took me a moment as the last of the fissure's energy disappeared to realize that I'd done it.

A cheer went up behind me and I turned, sharing a smile with Hobs and Sebille.

Hobs shot past me, through the door, before I could stop him. "No, Hobs!" I looked at Sebille. "I hope I did it right."

She rolled her eyes and stepped through after

the hobgoblin, Sadie chittering happily from her shoulder.

Wicked shot through next, and then I finally followed. Stepping into the familiar smells and sights and sounds of home, I smiled.

I looked at Sebille. "Please, goddess, let everybody be okay."

She pointed to the door. "Close it."

She was right. I needed to close and lock the breach before the real door would be there. Using my keeper magic to grab the knob as Sebille had done, I tugged it closed and created a ward to keep it closed.

Then I stood in front of the door, listening.

Silence met my desperate ears.

It was too quiet.

Not good.

I held my breath as I reached for the knob, my hand hovering over it as I checked for the painful heat.

It was perfectly cool.

Grasping the door, I yanked it open and stepped through.

I screeched to a halt, horrified. "No!"

"What's wrong?" Sebille stuck her head through over my shoulder, sucking in a gasp.

"It's not that bad," Grym said, glowering at us. He was almost unrecognizable under a gory coating of blood and guts and various substances that glued his dark hair to his head in thick tufts and coated his scratched and bloodied arms. Fortunately, he seemed mostly okay.

"I...I...I'm..." Words eluded me.

Most of the bookshelves were on the ground, some of them reduced to little more than kindling. The big window was shattered, glass glittering on the carpet and probably outside, judging from the violence of the destruction. Even the window frame was twisted, partially torn from the wall and hanging outside. Cold air slipped through the store, but I had a feeling the fresh breeze was a blessing, given the underlying stench that was a mix of sulfur, blood, rotting flesh, bodily waste, and dirty feet. The carpet had disappeared beneath a coating of material I probably didn't want to examine too closely. There were chunks of stuff that looked like bloody flesh and thick streaks of a slimy brown substance painted the walls. In the tea area, it looked like something had exploded. Green goo covered every available surface there. I squinted. "Is that an eyeball on a stick?"

"Don't ask," Grym said.

I looked up to find my beautiful copper tile ceiling bent and twisted, hunks of it missing completely. The perfect shape of a head was dented into the very center, complete with horns and what had probably been a pair of enormous ears. "Goddess," I breathed.

Rustin gave us a guilty smile. He looked a little better than Grym. I figured it was because he'd probably done most of his fighting from afar, using his prodigious magical skill instead of the brawn that was the gargoyle's trademark. "In our defense, you should have seen what came through that door."

A flushing sound preceded the opening of the bathroom door. Archie jerked to a stop in the door. His face was covered in a yellow-green substance, and there was a slimy pile of something that looked like poop on top of his head. His robes were ripped and filthy and there was a long, black mark down one side. Probably a scorch mark, since along with the assortment of other really bad smells, he stank of smoke. "There you are. How was it?"

I covered my nose. "You know, I'm starting to feel better about it."

Sebille barked out a laugh.

Hobs was sitting atop the only bookshelf that remained standing, heels kicking happily against the books. "Miss, they made a mess."

It was too much. I leaned against the frame and succumbed, laughter turning me into a shaking, tearful, gibbering idiot. When I could draw a breath without bursting into laughter again, I said. "It's really good to be home. Even if home looks like the site of a nuclear war."

The gargoyle, the witch and the sorcerer looked like they didn't quite believe me.

20

ICE CREAM, ICE CREAM, ICE CREAM

I spent the next week hiding in the library while the sounds of pounding, sawing, nailing, and general deconstructing and then reconstructing occurred on the other side of the door. I know it was cowardly, but I told myself I would only get in the way if I went in there.

Sebille and I had used the time to wrangle artifacts, and we'd made really good progress on that effort.

I was pretty sure the flow of new orders had slowed, which was good.

Sitting at Shakespeare's desk, I pulled the pile of artifact orders closer and sifted through them, siphoning the top four off the pile for the day's work.

A firm knock came on the dividing door, and I sighed. It had become a regular occurrence for me to be interrupted several times a day with contractor-type questions. I tried not to get too impatient with the questions. I was blessed that my insurance had covered most of the damage the battle had caused. It isn't easy to justify that kind of destruction to a company that would likely have me committed to an institution if I told them the devastation had been the result of monster infestation.

Yeah, that was a tight rope walk for sure.

In the end, Archie had offered to have a word with the insurance company, admitting that the Société was associated with the same company and he might have some pull.

It appeared that he had.

I grinned at the thought of how pretty my bookstore was going to be after the repairs.

Pulling the door open, I manufactured a pleasant expression for the burly guy standing on the other side. He was cute in an overly muscular way, and I wondered what type of magic user he was. Grym had called one of his cops who used to do construction work and asked for a reference. We'd thought it would be safest to have a supernormal crew. Just in case.

"Hi, Naida." The worker known only as Brad gave me a flirty smile and handed me a yellow envelope. "We found this when we pulled the counter out. It must have fallen down behind it."

I thanked him and closed the door, frowning at

the envelope. My eyes went wide when I saw the name on the return address.

Archibald Pudsnecker.

It was the elusive package he'd sent me. The one I'd thought I'd never gotten.

I tore the top off the envelope and started to pull the contents free.

Sebille trotted down the stairs. "You ready to go?"

I looked up from the envelope and hesitated. I really wasn't in a hurry to read about Archie's novels. Having met him, I had a feeling anything he wrote would be too strange for my tastes.

I made a quick decision, placing the envelope on the desk. "Yeah. I pulled four orders for today. Do you want to split up or go together?"

Sebille eyed the orders I handed her, zeroing in on the last one. Her gaze grew shrewd. "Let's split up, I'll take these last two."

I gave her wide eyes, knowing what she was up to. "Nice try. Let's go together."

Expelling a frustrated breath, Sebille slouched toward the door. "Okay, but I want to enjoy it one last time before we collect the artifact."

I thought about her request. It was appealing for more than one reason. "If we're doing that, we should bring Hobs."

Sebille grinned. "And Sadie."

I n the end, we brought Mr. Wicked and the frog too. We quickly knocked out the first two items on the list and then headed toward the Dairy Freeze ice cream shop.

Hobs was so excited at the idea of getting a chocolate hot fudge brownie sundae he could barely sit still. Sebille was hardly better than he was. She was sitting forward in her seat as if she could make the car go faster by leaning into it.

My cat and I were a united front of disgust at their juvenile behavior as we pulled into the lot. I stopped the bug, seeing no empty parking spots. "We might have to park on the street and walk," I told them.

Silence met my statement. I turned to find Sebille, Hobs, Wicked, and even the frog, who was perched on the dashboard, staring, unblinking at the giant ice cream cone sign hanging above the store on an oversized pole. The sign was an engineering marvel of lights and colors and movement that hypnotized the unsuspecting consumer into buying ice cream.

I'd suspected the first time I'd seen it that it was manipulating potential customers into buying ice cream. The artifact order in my pocket proved that I'd been right.

I stared at the monstrosity, my mind filled with

manufactured outrage, even while my will went all mushy and soft under its influence.

"I could really get behind a hot fudge banana boat with extra whipped cream," I told the car full of ice cream zombies.

They nodded without removing their gazes from the sign and climbed out of the car. I turned off the engine and got out too, leaving the car in the middle of the lot.

I could already feel the creamy sweetness of ice cream on my tongue.

Hey! What about me? said an outraged voice in my head. I'd forgotten Slimy! Shame filled me. I shook my head, dispelling some of the coercive effects of the sign. Looking back at the car, I knew I should go get the frog and move the car to a spot on the street.

But another little voice was chanting, *ice cream, ice cream, ice cream*, in my head. And I was helpless against it. "I'll see if they have fly-flavored ice cream for you," I promised the frog. Then I got into line with my friends.

We could always wrangle that sign tomorrow. Or next century.

The End

READ MORE ENCHANTING INQUIRIES

Did you enjoy **Croakies Monster**? If so, you might want to check out Book 9 of *Enchanted Inquiries*.

Please enjoy Chapter One of **Black & White Croakies**, as my gift to you!

Good parenting advice: Only allow your small frog, cat, and hobgoblin limited and supervised television time, or risk stunting their mental and physical growth.

Yeah, it might already be too late for that...

It seemed like good, innocent fun. A trip back to a simpler time, a fun jaunt to the "good old days". It turned out to be anything *but* harmless. The "kids" loved the old, black and white shows. But, per usual at Croakies, things devolved quickly, transforming "quiet" time into a heart-pounding adventure.

And of course, as you'd expect, the frog, the cat, and the hobgoblin are right in the middle of it all.

I'm a total derf at this whole parenting thing.

And my "children" are brats.

Holy flippin' frog flatulence. So much for the good old days...

BLACK & WHITE CROAKIES

"They're staring at that old TV again," Sebille informed me as she came into the bookstore from the artifact library.

I shrugged, secretly happy the terrible threesome wasn't flinging flour around the bookstore or creating more of those bunny-butted songbirds that had all but overrun Croakies. I'd had to hide the Plex hand vac from Hobs, my resident hobgoblin, because every time he used it to suck up dirt, the thing made more songbirds. They were currently lined two deep along the tops of my bookshelves, pooping all over the pretty new wood shelves beneath their feathered boohinds.

I had so many of the annoyingly happy critters in the store that I'd had to create a birdseed column in my monthly expenses.

"It's not hurting them," I said, the goddess of rationalization. "And it keeps them out of trouble."

"They need to turn it off and go use their imaginations or something," said the cranky sprite, whose parenting instincts had heretofore been inspired mostly by the pithy little sayings in the fortune cookies she so loved.

The tiny amalgamate dragon perched on Sebille's shoulder chittered happily, lifting her wings and flying across the room to visit with her friends the songbirds. The birds broke into happy song at the dragon's arrival. Little Sadie lifted her tiny head and joined them. Sebille and I winced. The dragon's "song" sounded more like screeching banshees than music.

Luckily, there were so many birds they mostly drowned the dragon out.

Silver lining.

A whistling theme song rose above the bird's clatter, as if Hobs was trying to drown out the happy noise by turning up the volume on the elderly TV. I recognized the song from a very old sitcom, which involved a country sheriff and his bumbling deputy dealing with a lot of silly problems.

Since I'd recently been lost in a dimensional wrinkle; had almost been killed by monsters, wizards, and demons more than once; and have had to continually deal with a naughty hobgoblin, a magical cat, and a snarky talking frog; I'd give almost anything to have problems such as, who was going to tell Aunt Bee her new rhubarb pie tasted like butt.

I'm just sayin'.

The door to my recently updated store opened, and a small elderly woman came inside, her eyes going wide as she took in the renovations. "Oh my! It looks lovely, dear."

I went over and embraced Mrs. Foxladle, my favorite human customer. "Thank you! It's so nice to see you. It's been a while."

Behind me, the dividing door closed softly. "Hello, Mrs. F," Sebille said, waving as she headed toward the tea counter. "Can I make you some tea?"

"No, thank you, Sebille dear. I won't be but a minute."

She squeezed my hand. "I've been a bit under the weather."

"Oh, no. Nothing serious, I hope?"

"Just a cold, dear. No worries. And then you were closed up for a couple of weeks." She looked around. "I barely recognize the place." Despite her kind words, her expression was dubious.

"I know it's shocking. But this old place was long overdue for a facelift." *Especially after being trashed by an epic battle against monsters from the abyss*, I thought. But, of course, I wouldn't tell Mrs. F that.

"I kind of liked its old, saggy face." She chuckled, reassuring me that her statement wasn't a criticism so much as a statement of fact. "When you get older like me, you find comfort in timeworn, familiar things. Do you know I've been coming to this wonderful store for twenty years?"

My eyes went wide. "Seriously?"

"Seriously." She gave me a mischievous look. "I'm glad you didn't replace that old sign outside. It always makes me smile."

I barely kept from rolling my eyes. I'd tried several times to update that stupid sign when I'd taken over Croakies. The scratched and tattered wooden sign with its ugly spotted frog was apparently under a magical grandfathering clause. Every time I'd tried to put a new sign in its place, or even change the name of the store, the sign had magically reappeared, and the paperwork had mysteriously reverted back to the old name.

I'd given up after several tries. I'd since decided to try to like the quirky ancient sign since it seemed I had no choice. "What can I help you with today?" I asked Mrs. F.

Her gaze skimmed away from mine as if she wasn't sure how her response would be received. "My visit isn't about books, dear. I know you occasionally take in...antiques."

Mrs. Foxladle had seen me with retrieved artifacts a time or two. I hadn't realized she'd noticed them or made a connection about my having them in my possession. The woman might be well into her seventies, but she was still sharp as a tack.

I shrugged, giving her a response that I hoped was suitably vague. "Occasionally, I help friends move things around."

"A friend of mine has been searching for a specific television set. An old black and white one. He collects antique entertainment media. I believe he has an old record player and a VHS player too." She shook her head. "Anyway, my friend Gladys walked by Croakies a couple of days ago and mentioned she'd seen you carrying one inside. I wondered if it was for sale?"

Black and white bat boogers! I suddenly felt like a bug under glass. Apparently, the whole city of Enchanted had been watching my every move.

I shook my head. "I'm sorry. That television belongs to a friend of mine. I'm just storing it for her until she moves into her new place." I really hated to lie to my favorite human, but I couldn't very well tell her the television was a magical artifact. The man we'd taken it from had been human and had apparently gotten it from my favorite giant.

Theopolis Gargantu owned Enchanted Collateral, Enchanted's only a pawn shop, and he'd apparently had the TV for a couple of decades, lost in the mess of his overstuffed home artifact.

What is a home artifact, you ask? It's pretty much as it sounds. A giant's residence is a living, breathing entity. A magical artifact. As such, it has a life of its own and you never know what to expect when you walk into one. Fortunately, like their owners, a giant's home artifact is generally benign. However, like the giants who live in them, the artifacts crave clutter and the accumulation of stuff. And that clutter always seemed to be moving around.

It would be easy for Theo to lose stuff in the clutter. In fact, he often did. The only miracle was that he ever managed to find *anything* in it.

When Theo's customer had come looking for the old relic, Theo had reluctantly decided to sell it to him. Only because the man had offered Theo several items in exchange for the TV. Apparently, as soon as he'd sold the ancient television, Theo'd had second thoughts, probably because he'd realized the man was human.

Selling magical artifacts to humans was a dangerous practice, against the laws of the magic governing body, the Société of Dire Magic. And if the Société found out that Theo had sold the artifact, he'd be in a lot of trouble. He might even lose Enchanted Collateral.

Which would all but kill him.

Anyway, when Theo realized the error of his ways, he'd come to me. He'd given me the man's address, and had reluctantly handed me an envelope filled with enough cash to buy it back. Sebille and I had gone to retrieve the television and found the man's door unlocked, and the television artifact on and showing only black and white snow on its small screen. There'd been no sign of the man, and, asking around, we'd gotten assurances by his neighbors that he hadn't been seen for a couple of days. So we'd taken the television form his living room and left the envelope in its place.

On the way back to Croakies, I'd called Detective Wise Grym to ask him to check into the man's disappearance. Which reminded me, I needed to check in with the handsome detective.

You know, just to find out if he'd located the man.

What other reason could I possibly have for calling him? Shush now.

"What's your friend's name?" Sebille asked, carrying a steaming cup of tea over and settling it on the brand-new table in the center of the open area at the front of the shop. Like most everything else, the previous table had been turned into so much kindling during the monster battle.

"Dugan McDonald," Mrs. Foxladle said, smiling shyly. "He's Irish."

Alarm tightened in my chest. I glanced at Sebille and found her widened gaze. That was the name of the man we'd taken the television from. "When was the last time you spoke to Mr. McDonald?" I asked Mrs. Foxladle.

She shrugged. "Last Sunday, I think. He goes to my church." She tugged her wool coat close around her throat as if she were cold. I realized when she spoke again that it was just nerves. She clearly liked the man a lot and was embarrassed to show it. "He has such a pleasant accent. So lilting. I believe there's romance in accents, don't you, dear?"

"Definitely. Are you sure you wouldn't like to stay for some tea?" I asked, hoping she'd take that as her cue to go. I needed to talk to Sebille about the new information and contact Grym.

"No. But thank you. I need to be going. Are we still on for book club tonight?"

I wanted to say no, but I didn't have the heart to disappoint her. I'd had to cancel her book club meeting for the last several weeks due to my busy schedule and then the renovations. I didn't want to let her down again.

"We're on for seven as planned. I might have to run out for a bit this afternoon, but I should be back in plenty of time."

She inclined her head. "Good. I'm really looking forward to it. Detective Grym has agreed to join us." Her smile was sly. I got the distinct impression the elderly woman had decided it was her job to fix me up with Wise Grym.

I had no intention of being the victim of her matchmaking. There was only so far I'd go to make a customer happy. Even one I liked as much as Mrs. Foxladle. "I'll see you tonight then."

I opened the door for her and found myself looking at the lean, rock-hewn form of the devil.

Or, Detective Grym.

Potato potahto.

Mrs. Foxladle beamed up at him. "There you are young man. We were just talking about you."

Grym took the hand she offered him and smiled down at the tiny woman. "No wonder my ears were ringing," he told her.

She laughed gaily. "We *will* see you tonight, won't we?"

"I wouldn't miss it for the world."

Watching him treat the elderly woman with such gentle kindness burned away another chunk of the anger I was still holding against the detective for outing me to the Société a few times. Yes, he'd just been doing his job when he'd reported some of my missteps as Keeper. But I hadn't been able to shake the feeling that he should have had my back.

Still, he'd stepped in to help me when I'd recently had a monster problem and he'd gone to bat for me with the Société when he probably shouldn't have.

He was slowly but surely worming his way into my good graces.

Grym watched Mrs. Foxladle walk away down the street and then turned to me, the pleasant expression on his handsome face sliding away. "We need to talk."

I pointed to the table where Sebille had been. It

was empty, but for Sebille's still steaming teacup. "Sit. Do you want tea?"

The sprite was already walking back to the table with two more cups. "I've got it."

Grym took his with a grateful smile and drank half of it in one gulp. I grimaced, wondering if his tongue was made of rock. That tea was hot. "Thanks, Sebille. What a morning."

I bit back the urge to laugh. "Worse than fighting a bunch of monsters escaping through a tear in the abyss?"

He smiled, shaking his head as he sipped his tea. "Not quite, but close." Grym set his cup down on the table and gave me an earnest look. "That television you picked up?"

I nodded. "You need to put it into the toxic magic vault ASAP."

I felt my eyes go wide. "Why?"

The detective scrubbed a big hand over his face, his gaze looking spooked. After everything he'd seen and done as a supernormal cop in a city that was filled with things like witches, dragons, wizards, and giant snake monsters, I wondered what could put that look in his dark-caramel eyes.

He met my gaze. Held it. "What did the living room of that house look like when you picked up the TV?"

Sebille and I shared a look. "Just like any other living room. A bit overcrowded and cluttered."

The sprite nodded. "It smelled like soup."

I wrinkled my nose. She wasn't wrong. It *had* smelled like cabbage soup. *Slug slobbers!* Not my favorite smell.

"It wasn't..." Grym looked down at his tea. I wondered at his hesitation to tell us what he'd seen. It was making me really nervous. My gaze slid to the dividing door, and I thought of that theme song that had suddenly blared from the back.

"Everything wasn't black and white?" Grym asked, his face flushing. "Like an old TV show?"

I shook my head. Sebille and I shared a look. "No."

Okay, leeching color from a house was concerning, I thought. But it didn't explain the haunted expression on Grym's handsome face.

"The color leeching was spreading as I stood there," he went on. "I tried to stay away from it, but it caught the tip of my shoe before I noticed."

He held his foot up so we could see the perfect line that separated the warm brown leather of his shoe from the flat, gray color of the toe.

"Yikes!" I said. "That's a bit concerning."

Grym shook his head. "That's not what's got me worried, though. I think that TV did something to McDonald." His haunted gaze lifted to mine. "I think it took him."

That took a beat to soak in. I sat there blinking at him.

Then horror hit, turning my spine to ice.

I surged from my chair at the same time the sprite did. I ran toward the dividing door and flung it open, surging through before I thought about what might be waiting for us.

The whistling theme song smacked us in the face like a fist. The sound was loud enough to lance my eardrums and make my head pulse.

I jolted to a stop, Sebille slamming into my back with a grunt. And stared around me in shock. The center of the giantnormous room was totally devoid of color. Everything within a circle of space was black, white, and gray. At the very center of that circle was the retrieved television artifact. But no ancient television show played across its screen. It was just snow. Black, white and gray spots dancing behind the curved glass face.

The floor in front of the television was empty except for the half-eaten remains of a frosted brownie.

And smeared along the edge of the old artifact, as if the person who'd been eating the brownie had tried to hold onto the frame to keep from being pulled inside, were several long smears of frosting. Like chocolate claw marks that screamed of fear and desperation.

Grym came up behind me as my knees buckled, my head shaking in denial. "No, no, no, no no..."

He caught me, holding me upright with a densely muscled arm around my waist. "Naida?"

Tears burned their way down my cheeks. "They're gone," I said, the words emerging thick and rough through my tear-clogged throat.

Without a word, Sebille reached over and clasped my hand in hers. "We'll get them back, Naida."

I just stood there shaking my head. Hobs, Wicked and Slimy were gone. Probably sucked into that stupid artifact. And it was all my fault.

I was a terrible parent.

"I should have made them go outside to play," I murmured, feeling as if my world had just crashed and burned beneath my feet. "I should have made them turn it off. I should have..."

Grym's arm tightened around my middle and it was the only thing holding me off the floor.

Check out the entire series here: https://samcheever.com/books/#enchanting

ALSO BY SAM CHEEVER

If you enjoyed **Croakies Monster**, you might also enjoy these other fun mystery series by Sam. To find out more, visit the **BOOKS** page at www. samcheever.com:

Enchanting Inquiries Paranormal Mysteries - **For more fun adventures with Naida, Sebille, Wicked, Slimy, and Hobs!**
Reluctant Familiar Paranormal Mysteries
Yesterday's Paranormal Mysteries
Gainfully Employed Mysteries
Silver Hills Cozy Mysteries
Country Cousin Mysteries

ABOUT THE AUTHOR

USA Today and WSJ Bestselling Author Sam Cheever writes contemporary and paranormal mystery and suspense, creating stories that draw you in and keep you eagerly turning pages. Known for writing great characters, snappy dialogue, and unique and exhilarating stories, Sam is the award-winning author of 80+ books.

To learn more about Sam and her work, visit her at one of her online hotspots:
www.samcheever.com
samcheever@samcheever.com